AMISH COUNTRY THREATS

DANA R. LYNN

D0035342

LOVE INSPIRED SUSPENSE
INSPIRATIONAL ROMANCE

LOVE INSPIRED® SUSPENSE
INSPIRATIONAL ROMANCE

ISBN-13: 978-1-335-72247-8

Amish Country Threats

Come unto me, all ye that labour and are heavy laden,
and I will give you rest. Take my yoke upon you,
and learn of me; for I am meek and lowly in heart:
and ye shall find rest unto your souls.
For my yoke is easy, and my burden is light.
—*Matthew* 11:28-30

To my children. I am blessed to be your mother.

Acknowledgments

There are so many people I want to thank!

Brad, I love you! This has been a crazy time, glad you're here with me. And thanks for all your knowledge about firefighters and EMTs! You were a great help!

Amy and Dee, my BFFs. I don't know how I'd survive without you and our coffee dates!

Lee Tobin McClain and Rachel Dylan, this journey has been so much better with you two! I love you guys and thanks for all the sympathy.

To my writing friends, there are too many of you to name, but I appreciate your wisdom and support.

To my street team, you ladies are awesome and I love you!

To Tina, my editor, and Tamela, my agent, thanks for your support and guidance.

Most important, to my Lord Jesus Christ, I pray that my words bring You glory. I am humbled to be Your child.

ONE

"Lilah!" Lilah Schwartz jerked awake at her brother Jacob's hoarse bellow. She tumbled from her bed and coughed as heavy, acrid smoke filled the air and coated her throat and nostrils.

Keep close to the floor. Crawling to the door, she ignored the splinter embedding itself in her palm. She struggled to breathe in as little as possible. Her bedroom was on the second floor. Even on her hands and knees, the air was thick with black smoke. Her eyes watered, stinging. Her airways shrank so small it felt like she was trying to breathe through a straw.

She reached the stairs and spun so she could crawl backward down the stairs. Lilah descended as quickly as she could without falling. Her limbs trembled, making movement awkward. Her lungs burned. She opened her mouth wide, gasping for air, but there was only smoke.

Gagging, she continued down the steps.

Jacob charged up the steps and grabbed her, hoisting her in his arms. His breathing was harsh and rasping in her ear. His arms shook as he carried her outside. The moment they hit the fresh summer air, she dragged in a deep lungful of oxygen. Jacob wobbled, then dropped to his knees, letting Lilah roll out of his arms and onto the dew-moistened grass. The sun was barely rising over the horizon. When he collapsed next to her, Hannah, his wife, ran over and begged him to get up. Despite her advanced pregnancy, she grabbed at her husband's arms and tugged.

Jacob opened his eyes and put a hand to Hannah's cheek, catching her tears. "I love you."

When she sobbed, he turned to Lilah. The glassy look in his eyes terrified her. She reached out and clutched his hand. Vaguely, she was aware of the neighbors hovering around them. Someone yelled that an ambulance was on the way. The men were working on halting the spread of the fire.

It didn't surprise her. Most of the people living in the eastern part of Holmes County, Ohio, were Amish. She'd lived in Sutter Springs, a borough tucked up against the thriving town of Berlin, Ohio, all her life. These people had known her and Jacob since they were born. They tended to help each other whenever the need arose.

Lilah kept all her focus on Jacob. He was all she had left since they'd lost their parents in a buggy accident six years earlier. Jacob had become father and brother to her. She couldn't lose him.

"Lilah," he rasped, his face ashen. "Not an accident. Buried. Go to office. It's there—"

He stopped, choking.

"What's in there? What am I looking for?"

Why was he thinking about his work now, when he needed to save his breath?

The ambulance arrived. Lilah watched them load Jacob into the vehicle. As the door closed, she held Hannah in her arms as her sister-in-law sobbed. She didn't realize it would be the last time she ever saw her brother.

Three days later, Lilah held her tears at bay as she sat stoically in the buggy, riding behind the simple pine casket holding the body of her older brother, the man who'd died saving her. How would she survive without him? He was all she had. Jacob had been the only constant in her life since their parents had died.

And now he was gone, too.

She sniffed, blinking to clear her blurred vision. No one knew how the fire had started. All the evidence had burned up with the large farmhouse. The place she'd lived her entire life was nothing more than rubble and ash. She and Hannah had left Sutter Springs and moved in with Hannah's *mamm* and *daed*. She appreciated the quiet of the small district but still missed her home. Twenty-nine years ago, her *daed* had built the *haus* for his new bride on the outskirts of Berlin, Ohio, a place known for its growing tourism. Growing up, her family had been far enough away to enjoy their privacy, but still had the option of hopping into their buggy and heading into Berlin and enjoying a day of visiting and shopping.

She sighed as she considered her new life. While Ben and Waneta Hostetler had been warm and considerate, Lilah had noted a new coldness in the way her sister-in-law treated her.

Maybe it was fear for the *boppli*. Although they didn't talk about such things, it was obvious to her that Hannah would soon give birth.

It would have been Jacob's first *boppli*. New tears threatened at the thought.

Her eyes slid to where Hannah sat beside her, holding the reins. Lilah had offered to drive, to allow Hannah a brief rest. The look she got in return could have frozen her where she sat. They hadn't spoken since.

Lilah didn't even have the distraction of school. For the past two years, she had taught at the Amish Elementary School in her district, but school had let out for the summer. Never had she missed the chaos and business of teaching as she did now.

The procession of mourners entered the cemetery. It was a fairly large cemetery as far as Amish cemeteries went. The back part of it was reserved for their Mennonite neighbors. All the graves looked the same. Plain wooden grave markers, with no distinction between them. Not even names. The plain markers were deliberately made so they would fade and become weathered.

It was the Amish way of showing that life on earth was passing.

It hurt her heart to think about it.

Hannah pulled on the reins, halting the buggy. Lilah wiped her eyes and scrambled off the seat. When she turned to assist her sister-in-law, Hannah ignored her outstretched hand and climbed down by herself.

Silently, the two women moved to the gravesite. They stood together. Yet Lilah had never felt more alone.

Lilah swallowed the large lump blocking her airway when the casket was lowered into the ground. Within minutes, it was over.

Hannah turned without a word and stumbled back to the buggy. Lilah followed. This time, she didn't offer her help, knowing it would be refused. She got back into the buggy and rode to Hannah's parents' *haus* with her.

At the *haus*, the neighbors kindly greeted Hannah and Lilah, offering their sympathy and telling stories about Jacob's life. The Amish tended to be practical regarding death. It happened to them all. Soft laughter rippled from across the room. Lilah stiffened.

She knew the women weren't being unkind. It was normal for mourners to visit and socialize at these times. Her bruised emotions were overly sensitive. Pivoting so they couldn't see her emotions, she noticed a man standing alone in the corner. That was odd. He held himself still, legs braced slightly, hands clasped in front of him. It was similar to the stance of the *Englisch* soldiers she'd seen on posters in town.

She blinked. His one hand looked slightly different. It took her a moment to realize it was a prosthetic arm.

His head turned and his brown eyes snagged hers for a moment before he looked away. She flushed. What was wrong with her? It was rude to stare, and he had caught her.

She needed some air. She grabbed her black bonnet from its peg on the wall and pulled it over her *kapp*. Walking briskly outside, she moved off the porch to breathe in the warm summer air to soothe herself and calm her racing heart.

"Lilah."

Lilah spun, her hand at her heart. She hadn't heard Hannah approach.

"Hannah, *geht es dir gut*?" Her sister-in-law appeared pale and wan. Not surprising, given the circumstances.

Hannah waved away her inquiry about how she was feeling with impatience. "I'm *gut*. Nothing wrong with me except that my *ehemann* is dead." Lilah cringed at Hannah's harsh words. "I wanted to talk with you."

She didn't like the tone in Hannah's voice. Ice dripped from each word.

"*Jah*, can I help you?" Lilah clenched her

hands into fists, hiding them in the folds of her black mourning dress to mask her distress.

"I'm sorry. I can't have you here anymore. I need you to find somewhere else to live."

"Your parents—"

"My parents have nothing to do with this. I'm the one asking you to leave."

Lilah stared at her. "Where would I go? You and Jacob were my only family."

Hannah shrugged, her eyes red from tears but steady. "I don't care. You can leave with one of the guests here. Anyone. I don't care who. I know what happened wasn't your fault, but my husband is dead because of you. If he hadn't gone back for you, Jacob would still be alive. I don't know if I can forgive you for that."

Shock burrowed into her. Lilah and Hannah had never been close, but they'd gotten along. The excitement of the coming *boppli* had seemed to draw them closer. Lilah had hoped they'd become sisters of the heart.

Now that hope was ashes at her feet. She couldn't blame Hannah. In fact, she agreed with her. If she had heard Jacob when he had first called out for her, she could have escaped without his help. He'd still be alive today.

Her heart was heavy in her chest. She

heard her brother's voice. Heard him telling her something was in his office. And that it wasn't an accident. What had he meant? Hannah started to turn away from her.

"Wait." She reached out to touch Hannah's arm. The other girl shrugged off her hand but stopped. Lilah dropped her hand, clenching her fists as she struggled to control the anguish swirling around inside her. She forced herself to continue speaking. "I need to grab something from the barn at my family's farm."

Hannah shrugged. "Take the buggy. It's early. You have time."

With a soft swish of her dress, Hannah turned and went back inside, leaving Lilah hollow and more alone than she'd ever felt. More alone than after *Mamm* and *Daed* had died.

Her feet took her to where the buggies were all parked, her mind hazy with shock. Where could she stay?

"I'm sorry about your brother." A deep voice behind her made her jump.

It was the man she'd noticed inside. The one she'd been staring at. His hair was blonder in the sun than it had appeared inside. The sympathy in his deep brown eyes nearly undid her composure.

She swallowed around the lump swelling inside her throat. *"Danke."*

"Do you need help?"

She shook her head. *"Nee. Danke."* She had to pause to steady herself. "I have to go find something."

A sudden flurry of activity near the barn caught their attention. When they looked, nothing was there. Probably animals, she decided. She turned back and found he was still watching her.

"I won't keep you, then. I wanted to tell you Jacob was a *gut* man."

"Jah. He was." Her eyes followed him. "How did you know him?"

He stopped and turned back to her. "I was one of his clients. More than that. He was a friend."

A lump swelled in her throat. "He'd wanted me to find something. At our *haus*. That's where I'm going," she said.

Why was she telling a stranger this? Lilah had always been a very private person. Something about this man, though, made her feel she could trust him with this burden. Ridiculous! She tightened her lips around the words hovering on her tongue. She couldn't confide in someone she didn't know, regardless of who he was to her brother.

He frowned, his gaze searching her face. He must have decided she wasn't going to say more. Nodding briefly, he turned and strode away. She should have asked for his name.

Rehitching the buggy, Lilah climbed up and grabbed the reins, directing the mare out onto the road. As she looked back, the *haus* vanished from sight. Unable to contain them any longer, she released the tears that had been dammed inside.

The journey from the Hostetler *haus* to where Lilah had lived with her brother and his wife took just under an hour. If Hannah had given her more notice, she could have hired a driver and made the trip in half that time. Pulling into the yard where her *haus* had stood less than a week ago, Lilah sucked in a deep breath to fortify herself. It didn't help. Weakness still sank in, making her legs wobble as she stepped down from the buggy.

Forcing herself to look away from the ruins of her *haus*, she strode into the small brown wooden shed connected to the barn, where Jacob had run his farrier business. Two steps inside the barn, she halted, her jaw dropping in shock.

Jacob had always been neat to the point of being obsessed. When she'd been in this office the day he'd died, he'd been in the middle of repairing the old cupboard on the back wall. She remembered there being a chain lock on it.

A chill slid up her spine, seeing it thrown to the ground, hacked open and splintered by some sort of tool. Looking around, she saw the maul leaning against the wall. That definitely didn't belong in here.

What was that noise?

Lilah held her breath as she heard footsteps out in the barn. Someone else was here. No one had reason to be here.

Her eyes flew to the shattered cupboard on the ground. Whoever was here had wanted something. Maybe even enough to kill for it.

She couldn't stay.

Carefully, she inched her way out of the office. The footsteps were close. Ducking into a stall, she waited. The steps entered the office.

This may be her only hope.

Running, she made it outside and climbed into the buggy. Flicking the reins, she ordered the startled mare to run.

A gunshot ripped into the back of the buggy. She couldn't take the buggy back to her sister-in-law's family. She'd already brought enough grief to Hannah. Another shot rang out.

Followed by the revving of a motor.

She knew she couldn't make it to safety in a buggy. Not on this paved road. Rounding a corner onto a narrow dirt path, she jumped down, then raced into the woods. The path was close enough to where she'd lived, hopefully someone would find the buggy and recognize it. Most of their friends and acquaintances knew where Hannah's family lived.

Lilah took off into the woods, running as fast as she could. Branches smacked into her face. She couldn't afford to slow down. Her right side burned. She wasn't used to this kind of exertion. Holding her hand to her side as if she could force the needle-sharp pangs away, she ran.

She didn't know how long she'd run before she came to a clearing. A *haus* she'd never seen loomed before her. She had a clear view of the back door and the side of the porch. Maybe she could knock on the door and ask for help.

She stepped into the clearing and hurried toward the structure. The revving of an engine broke into the silence. Just past the *haus*, through the tangle of tree branches, she saw a maroon truck. Was it whoever had shot at her?

Changing course, she bolted inside the nearest structure, a large barn. The odors of hay, manure and various animals assaulted her nostrils. Hunkering down, she leaned against the wall, her heart pounding like a jackhammer as she waited for whoever was following her to give up.

Who could it be? And why would anyone shoot at her?

Her mind flashed back to the night Jacob had died. He'd said the fire hadn't been an accident. She'd shied away from what he'd meant, that someone had set their *haus* afire. Someone had tried to kill them all.

And now he was coming after her.

Levi Burkholder should have offered to go with Jacob's sister. She had been holding on to her composure by a thread. He'd seen the agony in her stormy blue eyes, the way her throat worked as she struggled to converse calmly. When she had told him that she was visiting her destroyed *haus* to look for something of her brother's, he should have offered.

Except, she didn't seem to want his company. Her expression had closed the minute she'd said she was looking for something Jacob had told her about.

Still. He should have offered.

What a depressing morning. He'd attended far too many funerals, seen so many deaths, and he was heartsick. When the preacher ended the two-hour-long funeral ceremony today by stating Jacob's name, date of birth and date of death, it had struck Levi again how fleeting life is. Jacob had been a young man, younger than Levi. Only twenty-four, with a wife and a *boppli* on the way. And a young sister, who'd been devastated by his loss.

What would they do now?

Levi pushed the thoughts of her out of his mind. Amish communities were known for coming together and lending a hand when necessary. They'd be fine.

He clicked his tongue and touched the reins, maneuvering the buggy back into his barn, swiveling it back and forth to fit it into its narrow space. When it was settled into its proper place, he removed his gloves and set them on the shelf near the workbench. His left hand stung. A bee had climbed inside his glove and stung him. With his right hand, he used a flat blade to remove the stinger.

He was so used to the prosthetic arm that had replaced his right arm that he didn't have to think about how to make the fabricated fingers close around the blade.

He didn't mind his arm. It was a reminder that he was a survivor. In the most literal sense, having fought in Afghanistan. It was also a physical reminder to him of why he was thankful to be back in the Amish community he'd left when he was seventeen. Some days, though, he struggled just to fit back into the mold he'd thrown aside when he'd left. He'd been more than angry when he'd rejected the Amish life. He'd been betrayed. One of the elders had accused him of stealing. He hadn't. Never in his life had he taken anything that wasn't his. His *mamm* had listened. His *daed*, however, had believed the elder and had demanded Levi return the money and repent. They had often disagreed as Levi had grown up. This was the breaking point. The tenuous relationship unraveled, and Levi had left that night after a shouting match that burned a hole through his spirit.

A lot had happened to him since that time. He'd been a soldier, trained as a sniper, and had done and seen things that had left him broken and scarred. So broken, he knew he would never be whole again, regardless of whether he still had his arm. In his darkest moments, he'd realized he needed to come home.

That was several years ago.

Mamm had started trying to talk him into courting the neighbor woman. Miriam Zook was a fine woman, a widow with two sweet *kinder*. Levi had nothing against her. They had talked before. She was an intelligent, pleasant woman.

A woman who deserved more than he could give her. Levi had nothing to offer any woman. Afghanistan had left him with nightmares and flashbacks that he didn't know if he'd ever get past. Even though he had enjoyed talking with the widow, his heart had remained cold inside his chest.

A pair of dark blue eyes under a black bonnet swam before his eyes. He squeezed his eyes closed. Why was he thinking of someone he'd only just met? It was probably that he could identify with the sorrow in her eyes.

More than just his body had been broken by the war.

Sighing, Levi turned to enter his office.

A shuffling noise in the front of the barn caught his attention. It wasn't one of the cows his family owned. They were all out in the field and wouldn't come in until time to milk later that afternoon. Nor was it the goats. They were in the other barn. His mare was pastured in the back quarter of the fields.

Something was in his barn. Something that shouldn't be. He had to walk past it to exit. And he needed to do it now before anyone else in the family came into the structure.

Levi released the door latch and made his way to the front of the barn, instinctively stepping carefully and quietly as he'd been taught to do. The afternoon sun was no longer directly overhead but had started to shift to the west. It wouldn't set for hours, but as it streamed in through the windows in the rear of the barn, it cast long shadows across the floor.

Shadows that revealed that it was no animal trapped inside with him. It was a human.

Briefly, his hand twitched, wishing for the gun he'd carried for so many years.

Immediately he chastised himself. He was no longer a soldier. He'd been baptized into the Amish church. The Amish didn't believe in using guns against another person, not even to protect oneself. Guns were for hunting.

Clearing his mind, he focused on finding out who was hiding in his barn and why. He stepped closer.

A sniffle came from just beyond the first stall.

A sniffle?

Some of the tension drained from his shoulders. No longer bothering to mute his steps, he strode to the front and pulled the gate back from the stall. Crouching down inside, huge blue eyes staring up at him from a pale face, prayer *kapp* covered by a black bonnet, was a young woman in an unadorned black mourning dress.

A face he'd seen less than two hours ago.

He saw the scratches and scrapes on her face and hands, some of them smeared with blood. Those hadn't been there when he'd talked with her. Nor had she had such fear in her eyes. Something had gone very wrong since he'd last seen Jacob's little sister.

What had Jacob said his sister's name was? Lucy? *Nee.* Lilah.

"It's Lilah, *jah*?" She bobbed her head once, her gaze fearful. He softened his tone. "Why are you hiding in my barn?"

"I'm sorry," she gulped out, so low he leaned forward to hear her better. "I had nowhere else to go."

Levi scratched the back of his neck. Well, the sun was still up. It wouldn't take much to hitch up his mare. "Can I help you? Drive you back to the Hostetler *haus*?"

"Nee!" She bounded to her feet at the suggestion.

Panicked. That was the word for the look on her face. He hadn't seen anyone that distraught since his soldier days.

"Easy!" He lifted his hands. He was surprised that her gaze didn't veer toward his hand. He'd seen her staring at it earlier. Instead, her blue gaze remained on his face. He put the reaction aside. There were more important things to deal with now. "I'm Levi. Levi Burkholder. I met you earlier, remember? Your brother was my farrier. Would you let me help you? You're hurt."

He motioned to her scratches. Her hands rose to her face as if she hadn't even realized.

He continued to speak softly. "You don't want me to take you home? Won't your family be missing you?"

The terror in her blue eyes pierced the armor he'd built around his heart. He winced.

"I can't go home. Someone is after me. They shot at me."

His mouth dropped open. Now, that was unexpected. Hopefully she was mistaken. He took a step toward her. She cringed away from him.

"Look, I won't hurt you. You're hurt, and

you're in my barn. Why don't we go up to my *haus*? My *mamm* is home. She can tend to you. Maybe get you something to eat?"

She eyed him for a moment longer before nodding.

"Do you have a husband or any other family that I should notify?"

To his surprise, she shook her head. Most women her age were married. Jacob hadn't said she was married. He hadn't said she wasn't, either. All he'd said was his sister was the same age as his wife, Hannah. Levi kicked his curiosity aside. It was none of his business why she wasn't married.

When she stepped out of the stall, he saw that she was almost as tall as he was. Maybe three or four inches less than his own five foot eleven. The haunted expression on her face was too familiar. He'd seen it on soldiers in battle. It hurt him to look at her.

Averting his eyes from her, he opened the door and gestured for her to precede him out of the barn.

She hesitated for a moment, her huge eyes roaming his face. His face warmed under her gaze. He wasn't used to people watching him so closely.

He opened his mouth to try and convince

her when the sound of a motor coming over the hill reached his ears. All the color drained from her face.

She ducked back down inside the barn. "I can't let him see me!"

Levi poked his head out the door and watched a Jeep drive past. It was so covered in dirt and dust that he couldn't honestly make out the color. It could have been blue, gray or even green for all he could tell.

"Okay, look. The car is past. Let's go into the *haus*. I'll help you figure it out. *Jah?*"

He held the door open and waited. Something had her scared. He remembered her saying that someone was after her. Levi had seen too many innocent people suffer from the hands of others. A little more than five years ago, Sophie Forster, the wife of his best friend and former military buddy from the *Englisch* world, Aiden Forster, had been on the run with her young sister. He had helped Aiden rescue the two women. To this day, he shook his head at the thought of anyone wanting to harm Sophie or her spunky little sister, Celine.

He would not sit by and watch another innocent suffer.

He trained his eyes on the shaking figure in front of him. She was terrified. And alone.

He was honor bound to assist her. He might no longer be a soldier, but he would still honor the code ingrained in him.

Slowly, she stood up straight and said, "Jacob told me the fire that had killed him wasn't an accident."

Levi stared at her, the hair raised on the back of his neck. What had his friend gotten into?

TWO

Lilah didn't know what to do. This was the second time she'd crossed paths with this man in less than two hours. It struck her as odd that she'd found his barn to hide in. And the fact that he claimed to have been her brother's client? Jacob had mentioned a client named Levi. She couldn't be certain this was the same Levi. It wasn't an uncommon name, after all. And Jacob had never said his last name. If only she knew more about him. But she didn't. Jacob hadn't told her much about him. Her brother had always respected the privacy of other people. Especially his clients. She had gotten the feeling, though, that her brother had liked Levi.

She hoped this was the right man.

Her instincts told her she could trust him. She wasn't feeling too kindly toward her instincts at the moment. They hadn't prepared her for Hannah's telling her to leave.

Marvin King flashed through her mind. She flinched away from the memory of the young man who'd courted her last year. He'd courted her friend Ruth at the same time. Only later did she realize he'd been encouraging her affections while he was preparing to marry another. She'd lost her friend and her boyfriend the day she'd found out.

Nee, she couldn't trust her instincts where men were concerned.

Briefly, she considered the man standing in front of her, waiting for her to decide. Something about Levi, maybe the way he carried himself, made her confident that he could handle whatever came his way. That didn't mean, however, that she was comfortable explaining her situation to him. She didn't want to put him in danger any more than she had wanted to put Hannah in danger. Despite her sister-in-law's coldness, Lilah sympathized with her plight.

She didn't want to think about Hannah right now, nor did she want to talk to this stranger about being kicked out of her sister-in-law's home. Hannah was grieving. She hoped that within a few days, the other woman would reconsider and welcome Lilah back.

For now, though, Lilah was standing here, having been shot at and chased, with a man she'd never met before today who was asking her to trust him. Not likely.

But what choice did she have? Did the person who'd shot at her know that she had been staying with Hannah's family? It was possible. Anyone who knew their family would be aware that she had lived with Jacob and Hannah. It would make sense that she would go where her sister-in-law went. The fact that no one had showed up here waving a gun seemed to prove that the shooter didn't realize she was at the Burkholder place. For now. Maybe she could take some time to get her feet back under her again.

Her eyes met Levi's. The strength and patience in their depths steadied her more than any words could have.

"Please stay. Let us help you," Levi said.

Jacob had trusted him. She wouldn't let down her guard completely, but she'd let him help.

Deciding, she sucked in a deep breath to gain control of the emotions coursing through her before answering. She had to stay somewhere. It might be summer, but sometimes in

Ohio the nights got cold. And she felt a storm coming.

"I'll stay for a bit. Maybe tonight, *jah*? I'm too tired to think clearly, and I have no place else to go." Pushing away from the door, she moved closer to him. "I think my brother respected you."

A smile quirked his lips, then disappeared.

"It was mutual." He stepped back outside, motioning for her to wait, his hand down low. His eyes narrowed as they scanned the street, then the trees around them. There it was again. That posture that made her think of a soldier. "It's clear. Let's go."

Lilah hesitated only a second before following him out. She blinked against the sunlight. It boggled her mind that one of the darkest days of her life could be this bright and gorgeous outside. Her whole life had been turned upside down, yet the rest of the world kept moving.

Turning to look at him, her eyes zeroed in on the yard over his shoulder. She blinked a second time, this time to check and make sure she was seeing correctly.

"Is that a car?"

Actually, there were two cars there. Now, it wasn't odd seeing cars at Amish homes. She had a friend who received special education services from the local Intermediate Unit, a government funded facility that contracted with school districts to provide special education and training opportunities. Her friend had several therapists who visited her home each month. No, what was unusual was that both of these cars were obviously in the process of being worked on. One car was up on cinder blocks with all four wheels missing. The other one had an engine sitting beside it. The Amish didn't own automobiles.

"Jah." Levi shrugged, but didn't stop walking. "I don't own them. I just fix them. I'm *gut* at fixing things."

"Isn't that *verboten*?" She couldn't imagine her bishop allowing anyone in their district to work on cars.

"My bishop approved it. I'm allowed to work on cars and drive them in my dealings with *Englisch*." He slanted his eyes her way. "He knew that's how I made my living when I was in the *Englisch* world. It was a trade I knew and did well, even with my arm."

She nodded. His bishop was more lenient than hers. She knew that rules could change from one district to another.

He opened the back door of his *haus* and

gestured for her to walk inside. She stepped into the large, airy kitchen, bright with natural light streaming in through the large windows. The center of the room was taken up by a large wooden table surrounded by six wooden chairs. There was a plain white cloth covering the table and no cushions on the seats.

"Levi? *Bist du das?*" A thready feminine voice called from the next room.

"*Jah, Mamm.* I'm home. I brought a—" He glanced at Lilah awkwardly. "Um, I have a friend with me."

A chair creaked in the other room. Levi jerked at the sound and strode to the door, waving for her to follow. "*Nee, Mamm.* Don't get up. This is Lilah Schwartz."

Lilah found herself under keen scrutiny from a fragile-looking woman sitting in a chair, her fingers slightly gnarled and knuckles swollen. Fragile she might have been, but there was strength in that glance. She knew the woman hadn't missed anything about her appearance.

"Lilah, this my mother, Fannie Burkholder."

"Lilah." The older woman pursed her lips and tilted her head. "I can't remember you mentioning a friend named Lilah before."

"I have mentioned her brother, Jacob Schwartz."

The instant she heard the name, Fannie's face softened. "*Ach.* I heard about the fire. Levi, you went to the funeral today, *jah*?"

He nodded. "I did. *Mamm*, we—I mean, Lilah has a problem."

She saw his mother's sparse eyebrows climb up her forehead. Curiosity sparked in her eyes. When she turned those brown eyes, so like her son's, on Lilah, she fidgeted, her face flushing. How was she supposed to describe what was happening in her life? She hadn't told Levi everything. Part of her worried that they would think she was making things up.

Ach. How much should she say? Not only did she not want to sound foolish but Lilah was also a private person. She wasn't comfortable telling near strangers about the coldness that had developed between herself and Hannah. Nor did she want their sympathy for what she'd been through.

What choice did she have? Her brother had wanted her to find something. It was important. If only she knew why.

"What's your problem, Lilah?" Fannie questioned when the silence had stretched into nearly a minute, her voice kind and motherly.

There it was. She could deny having a problem. Her privacy would be protected, but she would still be without a place to stay, and with questions building up inside. Questions that she needed answers for, not only to honor her brother's request but also because she didn't know if she'd ever be safe again until she found out what was happening.

Swallowing her pride, she drew in a deep breath. Her stomach was quivering inside her like the Jell-O molds she sometimes made for her students as a treat. She crossed her arms over her belly to hold the trembling inside. Where to begin?

Her eyes flicked upward. Levi nodded at her, his face calm. And kind. Something in his expression anchored her, gave her courage. She had to tell someone.

Outside on the road, a vehicle passed. Was that the person trying to kill her? She fought not to cringe. No one could see her inside the *haus*. She was safe for now.

But how long would she remain safe if she didn't find out who was after her and why?

What could be worth murder?

Levi took a single step toward her before he pulled himself to a stop. The struggle on her face tugged at his heart. But he knew there was nothing he could do for her. He kept hearing her saying someone was after her, but he didn't know anything more. He needed details, which only she could give.

Settling back into his at ease stance, he deliberately caught her gaze, trying to impart his support to her without words. When the tension dancing across her shoulders quieted, the knot inside him settled. Mentally, he prayed for peace. Then he waited.

"Three nights ago," she began in a voice just barely more than a whisper. He leaned forward to hear better. "I was asleep when my brother yelled for me. Our *haus* was afire. I couldn't get out fast enough. Jacob, he had gotten Hannah out. His wife. Then he came back for me." A tear slowly tracked down her cheek, but Levi didn't think she was aware of it. "When we got outside, he collapsed. He'd inhaled too much smoke."

He could see it in his mind. Blended with that was a scene of a comrade falling after saving his life. He wrenched his mind away from that, sweat beading on his forehead. With effort he refocused on Lilah. He couldn't afford to let himself get trapped in those memories. It was bad enough that he couldn't escape them while he slept.

Lilah had fallen silent. "Lilah?"

She jerked slightly. "He said it wasn't an accident. That I needed to find something in his office."

A chill swept through him. "What wasn't an accident?"

Her fearful gaze rose to meet his. "I don't know. I'm scared to find out."

Was it the fire? Did Jacob suspect arson? Or worse?

Or had he been involved in something else?

Levi recalled the last time he'd seen his farrier. Jacob's easy smile had changed. He'd been cagey. His hands had shaken. He'd dropped tools twice. Jacob had never dropped a single tool in the years he'd known him.

Something had changed. Something that had put him on edge.

"Did you talk to his wife about it? You're staying with her family, *jah*?"

As he asked, he frowned. Why hadn't Lilah returned to Ben and Waneta's *haus* when she got scared?

A current of red swept up Lilah's neck and pale face. Her gaze dropped. "I can't go back there. Hannah, Jacob's wife, asked me to leave."

Silence followed her words. Broken when

Fannie sniffed, the sound loud in the quiet room, reeking of disapproval. Lilah stiffened.

"I don't blame her." Lilah's chin rose, though there was still a tremor in her voice. "*Nee*, I don't. She lost her husband. I'm a reminder of why he's gone. She needs time to heal. We all do."

"*Jah*, but to ask you to leave…" Fannie shook her head. "You were mourning, too. Soon, the community will get together to re-build her *haus*. Maybe you could go back then, ain't so?"

Lilah didn't argue, but Levi saw the doubt flicker across her face. Levi wouldn't let himself get distracted. As much as he wanted to comfort her, he knew there was more. "What else happened?"

He winced as his *mamm* glared at him. If he'd been next to her, she would have elbowed him. But he wouldn't give in. He needed to know if there was a danger to his family that he needed to watch for. He had already decided that she would have refuge at his *haus* if he could provide it.

"I took the buggy to Jacob's office. I didn't know what he had there, or if I would recognize what he wanted me to locate, but I had to try."

He nodded. He would have done the same thing.

"When I got there…" She stopped and buried her face in her hands for a moment, shuddering. He waited. She dropped her hands, her expression resolute. "When I got there, his office had been messed up. His things thrown everywhere. I heard someone else in the barn."

"The barn is attached to his office, *jah*?"

"Jah. I ran to the buggy. He must have seen me. He shot at me."

Fannie gasped.

"Did you see him?" Levi demanded. When she flinched at his harsh tone, he could have kicked himself. "Sorry. I'm not yelling at you. But if you could identify him…"

Would they go to the police? He knew his parents wouldn't recommend involving *Englisch* law enforcement, but in a case like this, it was most likely an *Englischer* who'd been shooting at her.

"Nee. I heard an engine and knew I had no chance of escaping in a buggy. So, I abandoned the buggy and ran through the woods. When I saw your *haus*, I thought of coming to the door for help. But someone was driving on the road…"

"You thought it might have been the man

who'd been shooting at you." He finished her thought, frowning. "That's why you were hiding in the barn."

He couldn't get the image of her huddled down, pale and shaken, out of his mind.

"Jah."

"We have a busy road here." Fannie lifted a hand to gesture toward the front window. A pickup truck was passing. Two seconds later, a small sedan passed the *haus* from the opposite direction. "We're on the tourism route."

Lilah made an alarmed sound. Levi moved closer to her. "We're not part of the tourist attractions," he clarified. "No one stops here. Two doors down, the family runs a store from their *haus*. The tourists stop there."

"Jah. My Levi drives tourists around in a buggy," Fannie said.

He hadn't planned on mentioning that. Some folks didn't like the tourism. His parents didn't agree with it completely but had accepted that it was the way things were. Lilah blinked in surprise, but other than that, he could discern no reaction. He didn't allow himself to linger on why her disapproval would have bothered him. He was earning an honest living. He wasn't ashamed of it.

"Well, you'll stay with us tonight, *jah*?" Fannie struggled up from her seat, waving away Lilah's offer of assistance. "*Nee*, I'm fine. I'm going to start dinner. Lilah, you stay here and rest. You've had a rough day."

Levi knew better than to try and coddle his mother. She suffered from rheumatoid arthritis but didn't like to let it slow her down. Some days were worse than others. Today was a good day.

"Just a moment." Levi followed his mother to the kitchen. He pitched his voice low to keep Lilah from hearing him. "Are you sure, *Mamm*? I want to help her, but this is your *haus*."

He hated adding to her workload. Fannie Burkholder had the gift of hospitality. She'd go out of her way to make Lilah feel welcome. Nor would she complain of pain, even if she had trouble walking or completing simple tasks.

Fannie patted his cheek. "*Ach*. You worry too much, my *sohn*. *Gott* brought that young *maidal* here. We will not turn her away."

He nodded his head. It never failed to amaze him, the strength of his mother's faith. He had been questioning his for so many years. Even after he had repented and returned to the community where he was raised, he struggled to turn things over to *Gott*. Levi had gotten used to handling his problems on his own.

Returning to Lilah, he sat in the chair his mother had vacated. "My *daed* and my two younger brothers will be home within an hour. Do you need to rest before dinner?"

His father was the one person who might object, but he didn't think he would. David Burkholder was a *gut* man. Despite the issues that had driven a wedge between them, Levi respected his father and believed he'd try and do the right thing.

She leaned forward. "I don't need to rest. I need to plan. Levi, I think the person who shot at me wants whatever my brother had hidden in his office. I have no idea what it might be, but I need to find it. I have to know what happened and why."

"It's too late to do anything today."

"Maybe so. But tomorrow, I will go back to the office to look around."

He shook his head. "*Nee*. Tomorrow is Sunday. On Monday you can start your search."

Although, not by herself she wouldn't. Levi ignored the stray thought that he should mind his own business. Too many people in the community knew about his past and doubted his commitment to the Plain way of life.

Nee, he couldn't back away. Jacob was his friend. But more than that, Levi was not a man who would allow a young woman to walk into danger alone.

She hissed between her teeth. It didn't go over well to be told she had to wait. She didn't argue. The Sabbath was a day of rest. She'd have to wait. Whether she wanted to or not.

"I'll go with you." He hadn't meant to blurt it out like that.

She frowned at him. "I appreciate the offer, but I'm already inconveniencing your family enough."

He shook his head. "It's no inconvenience. You're my friend's sister. I want to find out what happened to Jacob."

And stop whoever was coming for Lilah. He'd put whatever fascination he had with the pretty blonde aside and help her. For her brother's sake. Whoever was after her, they'd have to get through him.

THREE

David Burkholder arrived home as Fannie
was putting the finishing touches on their supper. Her happy chatter filled the room, sup-
plemented by Lilah's soft responses. David's
glance shot to the young woman in a black
mourning dress setting the table. Lilah had
persuaded Levi's *mamm* to allow her to help,
claiming it would take her mind off her troubles to keep busy. Levi appreciated her easing
his *mamm*'s burden. He kept out of their way.
While they worked, he had gone to the front
window several times. He wasn't sure who or
what he was watching for, but he couldn't ignore the gut instinct warning him that danger
was coming. In his experience, if someone had
shot at Lilah once, there was nothing stopping
them from shooting at her again.

He returned to the kitchen to find that his

mamm and *daed* had stepped outside onto the steps. Shallow trenches lined Lilah's forehead.

"Don't worry," he whispered.

She tossed him a tight smile but didn't relax. When his parents returned to the kitchen five minutes later, she hid her hands in the folds of her apron. Not before he saw the way they trembled. The urge to go to her and take her hand startled him. His *daed* greeted her solemnly. When his brothers walked into the *haus* and hung their hats on the hooks lining the wall, his *mamm* introduced her as a friend of Levi's. A very brief description of her troubles was given to Abram and Samuel. Abram at twenty-three was almost four years younger than he was. He'd recently started walking out with a young woman, and the family was confident they'd be announcing plans to marry in the fall. Levi had his doubts. Abram didn't strike him as a man in love. Samuel was nineteen and hadn't started courting anyone seriously yet. Levi also had two sisters, Esther and Barb. They'd both married and left home.

Levi turned his head in time to see his youngest brother sneaked several peeks at their guest. Levi caught his eyes and frowned.

Sam shrugged as if to say, "What do you expect?"

Levi understood. Lilah was lovely, even in mourning.

As he'd expected, his father didn't make a fuss about having a houseguest for a few days. What Levi didn't expect was how well his family accepted the fact that he was going to go with her to search the office on Monday morning.

"Would you like me to come?" his brother Abram offered. Samuel quickly followed suit.

"Danke, nee." He declined the offer. Abram and Sam both had other responsibilities. Besides, Jacob had been *his* friend. Not to mention, he had made a promise to Lilah.

Levi always kept his promises.

The conversation at dinner was muted. Lilah left to go to bed as soon as the meal ended. Levi headed to his own room later that night, his mind whirling with questions. What had Jacob gotten himself into?

Whatever it was, it was bad enough to cause someone to want to kill. His sleep was uneasy, interrupted by dreams of explosions and shellfire. After jerking awake from a particularly disturbing nightmare, he gave up on sleeping.

Sunday passed in a quiet haze. Their community held church every other week. It moved around to a different family's *haus* each time.

Last week had been a church week. Off weeks were typically for visiting or courting.

After breakfast, Levi's *mamm*, *daed* and brothers left to go visit his *aenti* and *onkel* and their children.

"Are you sure you won't *cumme*?" *Mamm* picked up the pie and the fresh bread she'd made for her sister. Her knuckles were swollen this morning.

Levi kissed her forehead and swiped the baked goods from her arms to carry them to the buggy. "*Nee, Mamm*. I don't want to leave Lilah alone. She needs some quiet time to grieve and to think."

Mamm cupped his cheek with her hand. Only she could treat him like a kid and not be irritating. "*Jah*. You are a *gut sohn*."

Levi stood on the porch and watched the buggy turn out of the driveway. He went back into the *haus* to find Lilah. She was standing in the front room, staring out the large picture window, her arms crossed over her stomach. Stepping up close to her, he squelched the sudden urge to run his fingers over the faint lines digging into her forehead to try and smooth them out.

That would not be appropriate.

"Lilah…" He stopped, not knowing what he could say.

The corners of her lips tilted in such a pitiful attempt at a smile, his chest ached.

"I'm fine, Levi. I just can't believe he's gone. You know?"

He nodded. He knew the feeling well.

"He's all the family I had left. My *mamm* and *daed* had moved here from Illinois nearly thirty years ago, before either Jacob or I were born. I've been to Illinois to visit family twice, but I haven't seen any of them for years. Then five years ago, we were in a van, driving somewhere—I don't remember where— when a drunk driver hit the vehicle. Our driver, *Mamm*, *Daed* were all killed. Jacob and I survived, but both of us had severe injuries. After we left the hospital, our *haus* was too big, until Hannah moved in. Now it's all gone."

He knew the emptiness she was feeling. There was nothing he could do but listen. In time, she'd heal. Hopefully. It was in *Gott*'s hands.

Thunder was rumbling close by. As the minutes ticked by, he could hear it growing closer and closer. Levi gave up trying to sleep. His rest had been disturbed by echoes of the story Lilah had told him yesterday.

He might as well get up and watch the coming storm.

Levi had always been fascinated by weather, its power and its quicksilver changes. Well, he wasn't sleeping, so he might as well go watch. Leaving his room in his socks, he strolled to the kitchen. It was still pitch-dark out. Turning the natural gas lantern on low, he started some coffee, then dressed and put his boots on while it percolated on the stove. When it was ready, he poured himself a mug and took a sip of it. Just the way he liked it. Strong and black. Lilah padded into the kitchen as he was grabbing his hat. From the pinched look around her eyes, she hadn't slept much, either.

"Coffee, if you want it." He gestured toward the pot with his mug.

Nodding, she grabbed her own mug and poured herself a cup.

"I'm going out on the porch to watch the storm. Join me?"

"Might as well."

He watched as she pulled her bonnet on, hiding the bit of honey-blonde hair that wasn't covered by her prayer *kapp*. She had beautiful hair.

He shook his head to clear it of such irrelevant thoughts. He had no business noticing that.

When she had her coffee, they moved to the porch. Sipping the bitter liquid, they stood side by side, without speaking, as the fierce storm moved overhead. Thunder crashed, so close the wooden floor beneath their feet vibrated. Lightning flashed, illuminating the darkness for a brief moment before flickering out. In the distance, there was a creak and a resounding crack as a tree branch broke under the driving force of the wind.

"Let's leave as soon as morning chores are done," he said.

Another flash of lightning showed her lips flattened into a straight line for a moment. She didn't want to wait. Would she argue?

"I don't want to go over until the storm is through, anyway," he continued. "It will be easier to leave in a hurry if the roads aren't all wet."

A sigh escaped from Lilah. "*Jah*. You're right."

He grinned in the dark. She sounded as though the agreement had been wrung from her. As long as she agreed, though, he wouldn't complain.

As soon as they heard his parents stirring inside, they turned to go back into the *haus*. Levi held the door open for Lilah, inhaling as she went past him. Even after spending years away from the Amish community, he appreciated the lack of perfume or artificial fragrance.

Lilah paused halfway inside the *haus*. "*Danke*, Levi. For helping me."

It was almost ten in the morning by the time they managed to leave. The tension simmering around Lilah was nearly tangible. Her hands were clasped demurely in her lap as she sat next to him on the bench, but her knuckles were white. She held her back ramrod straight.

He scoured his mind for something light to say to break the silence but came out with nothing. What could he possibly say? Her brother was dead, and she had to know that it was starting to look like murder. Didn't she?

He focused on getting her to her brother's office. When he pulled off the main road onto the dirt road leading to her *haus*, the buggy lurched slightly as the pavement dropped off. Lilah grabbed the bench with both hands to steady herself.

"Sorry. I forgot how bumpy that spot was." He needed to pay attention to the road and not let her presence distract him.

"I'm fine. I wasn't paying attention, or I would have been better prepared."

A car was heading toward them. Lilah tensed beside him when the vehicle started to slow down.

"It's okay. I know this guy. Billy Whitman. He owns one of the cars I'm working on. He also did business with your brother."

Her posture loosened next to him, but she was still uneasy.

"Hey, Levi." Billy looped his elbow out the window, his right hand resting carelessly on the wheel. "Funny seeing you all the way out here. I was planning on stopping by later to check on my ride."

Lilah blinked at that. "He means his car," Levi murmured to her.

"It'll be ready in five days. I have to work Saturday morning, so I'll leave the keys and the invoice on the dashboard, okay?"

"That's perfect." Billy tilted his head to get a better look at Lilah. "Hey, I didn't know you had a girlfriend."

Lilah's eyes grew wide before she averted her face, flushing.

"I don't," he responded, not liking the taste of regret in his mouth. "This is Jacob Schwartz's sister."

Instantly, Billy's grin vanished. "Oh, hey. Sorry about that. Miss Schwartz, Jake was a good guy. I'm sorry for your loss. Have you heard if they've caught the person responsible?"

Lilah stared at Billy. "I don't—I'm not sure what you mean? Responsible for what?"

"For the arson."

Levi and Lilah exchanged shocked glances. "Are you sure it was arson, Billy?"

Levi didn't really doubt it, but he didn't want to trust Billy's information. The man was not the most reliable source. He tended to go by the theory that if it was on the internet, or if someone said it, it had to be true. However, this did confirm what Jacob had told Lilah before he died.

Now Billy scoffed. "I was talking to one of the firefighters who came to the scene the night of the fire. He's a neighbor. It was declared arson. I can't believe you didn't know it. The report was given to the wife two days ago."

Lilah had gone so pale, Levi feared she might pass out. He needed to get her out of here. Fast. Levi pulled on the reins to get the mare's attention. "Billy, you stop by when you need to get your car. I'm on a schedule today, so I need to go."

"Oh, yeah. Great talking to you, man. Take care."

As Levi flicked the reins, Billy took off, his tires spitting dust and gravel. Levi glanced back at him. At the corner, Billy turned to look in their direction again. Suddenly, the friendly grin he'd worn was gone. In its place was a glare. And it was directed at Lilah.

At his side, she gasped. She'd seen his glare, too.

"Come on. Let's go look in the office and then go home. Something's going on and I don't like not knowing what it is."

Lilah was only too glad to continue on their way. Her *haus* had been destroyed by arson? She'd wondered about it. What else could Jacob have meant? But hearing it confirmed was like watching her brother die all over again. Her faith was a brittle thread, frayed and fragile. Her mind switched to the look Billy had shot at her. Why was he so angry? They'd never met before. At least, she had no memory of ever meeting him. He had changed so fast, like a chameleon switching colors. What could it all mean?

That wasn't what bothered her the most, though.

"Hannah knew." She hadn't planned on blurting her thoughts out loud, but it was too late to pull them back in. "I don't know why she wouldn't have told me about my *haus*."

Levi was silent for a moment. "Maybe she was protecting you."

"Protecting me." She opened her mouth to speak, but then a new horror occurred to her. Someone had killed her brother. They'd set her *haus* on fire when she, Jacob and Hannah had been inside, uncaring that multiple lives could have been lost that night. The grief swamped her, and she started sobbing. It was hard to draw in a full breath.

Levi stopped the buggy and waited until she was done. Weak, she allowed herself to·lean against him for a moment.

"Someone killed him."

The sound of her own voice saying the words nearly made her break into tears again. Her eyes were gritty and raw from tears, her throat scratchy.

"*Jah*. I know."

She moved her head so she could get a better look at him. His face was grim, the eyes steady. Again, the image of a soldier crept into her mind. Which was silly. Amish men were not soldiers. They were pacifists. They used guns to hunt and provide for their families. Never to kill, not even to protect themselves or their families.

"You already knew, didn't you?"

"I didn't know for sure, but it seemed likely. This is one time I didn't want to be right." He glanced into her eyes. "You knew, too. You didn't want to believe it, but you knew."

She hated that he was right. Her pulse sped up. "Levi, do you think that Jacob was killed for whatever he had hidden in his office? Was that why our *haus* was burned down?"

"Could be."

"I can't think what else he could have meant." He hesitated for a moment.

"What? Tell me?"

"Lilah, had you noticed any changes in Jacob lately?"

Her back straightened and she narrowed her eyes to slits. "What are you trying to say, Levi Burkholder?"

He warded her off with his hands upraised. "I'm not saying anything. I'm asking a question. Had you noticed a change?"

She wanted to deny it. So much. She opened her mouth but stopped. No matter how it pained her, she had to be honest. "*Jah*. I noticed a change. He seemed to be worried. Anxious. I thought it was because of the *boppli*."

Realizing what she had said, her face burned. One did not speak of such things. Her brother and Hannah hadn't mentioned that Hannah was expecting. Lilah was able to see it for herself, but very few people talked about such a thing until the *boppli* was born. She quickly diverted the subject back to his original question. "Had you? Noticed a change?"

He nodded. It knocked the wind out of her like a fist to the gut would have. "*Jah*. I don't know what it means, Lilah. Maybe it's like you said. He was worried about—um—other things. Maybe he had gotten himself into some kind of trouble. I don't know."

"Something else," she said slowly, her mind sorting through other hints she'd missed at the time. "Jacob had a few out-of-town meetings in the past few months. That was new. Previously, all his business had been local."

His face stilled. His eyes narrowed and he frowned, as if he were trying to solve a complex problem in his head.

Lilah waited. Levi didn't speak. She fiddled with the string of her *kapp*, looping it around her finger and tugging at it as she waited. Shifting on the bench beside him, she resisted the urge to prompt him. Patience had never been her strength. It was worse now. She wanted answers and she wanted them immediately.

Finally, he spoke. "I don't know what was going on, but all my instincts are screaming that Jacob had gotten himself into something bad. Possibly illegal."

Her brother, Jacob? She shook her head. "*Nee.* I can't believe that. My brother was always honest and kind."

She met his gaze and flinched. Although sympathetic, the unwavering intensity of his brown eyes seared through her. "Kind people make mistakes like everyone else. They just have different motivations."

What could have motivated Jacob to do anything illegal? Something that was bad enough that it got him killed, and nearly killed the rest of his family? She fought back the familiar wave of grief and regret. If she survived this mess, there'd be plenty of time to dwell on how Jacob might have survived if not for her.

"We have to find whatever was in his office." She turned to Levi for confirmation.

"*Jah.*" He nodded. "I agree. It must have been something serious if those were his last words to you."

Levi started the mare trotting again.

"What if someone decided to burn his office, too?" she wondered out loud, wrapping her arms around her waist. Despite the sun pounding down on them, she shivered. "The man who shot at me had been going through Jacob's office."

"Lilah."

She glanced up at his deep voice.

"Don't borrow trouble," Levi advised. "We'll do everything humanly possible to figure this out."

She nodded but couldn't stop the thoughts twisting through her mind. "I wonder if Hannah had anything to do with it." The words were out before she'd thought them through.

That got a reaction from him. "Hannah? Your brother's wife? That Hannah?"

She rolled her eyes. "*Jah*, that Hannah. Or even Billy."

He didn't scoff, as she'd feared he might. "Billy Whitman. Hmm. Before today, I would have laughed at the thought. But I saw the way he glared at you. I've never seen that side of him before."

She shivered as she recalled Billy's cold glare when he thought she wasn't looking. She was so deep in thought, it startled her when

Levi pulled the reins sharply and stopped the buggy. She looked up to make a sharp remark. Instead, her jaw dropped open at the sight in front of her.

The shed where Jacob had worked, the place they needed to search, was nothing more than a pile of splintered debris under the weight of a thick oak tree, which had fallen. That oak had survived hundreds of storms worse than last night's.

Her mind couldn't process what she was seeing. Had the storm knocked it over? It didn't seem possible.

"There are no other branches or trees down." She barely recognized that hollow voice as hers. "How could the storm have knocked this one down?"

Levi didn't answer. He stepped down from the bench and strode to the edge of the debris. She scrambled down after him. Everything was a mess. There wasn't a single board of the building that hadn't broken when the tree crushed it.

"It wasn't the storm."

"What?"

Levi had walked over to the tree stump. "The storm wasn't that strong. None of the smaller trees are down. Nor are there any dead branches." He picked up a branch. "Look. See how green these leaves are? And look at the wood. This was a healthy tree. Unless there was a tornado, it should have survived."

"True."

"*Cumme.* Look at this."

She stepped around a gopher hole and joined him, squatting next to him. He reached down and scooped up a handful of fine, light brown shavings. Her mouth went dry. "This is sawdust. This tree wasn't broken by the storm. It was deliberately cut down to keep you out of the office."

She shook her head. "What was my brother involved with?"

"I don't know. But I think whoever killed him did this. And I think that person wouldn't think twice about killing anyone who got in their way."

FOUR

Lilah shuddered and squeezed her eyes shut, her arms wrapping around her middle. Seeing her chin start to tremble, Levi berated himself for speaking so bluntly. He had always been plainspoken. His time in the military had only sharpened that trait. As he wasn't a very sociable fellow, Levi didn't often worry about what he said. His family knew him well enough not to be offended by anything that came out of his mouth.

Not that he was rude. He just tended to speak his mind. At least he had cleaned up his language since he left the service. The rough language of some of his comrades had never stuck with him. He might have been a rebel, but there were some parts of his upbringing that he couldn't shake, even at his worst.

Reaching out his left hand, he tentatively placed it on her shoulder. "I'm sorry. I didn't mean to upset you. Sometimes I don't think before I speak."

Those blue eyes opened and speared him. He felt that glance deep in his soul. There was no judgment or disgust, only a bleakness that struck him like a physical pain.

"I'd rather you tell me the truth than lie to me," she whispered, her voice raw. "Even if the truth you tell me isn't one I want to hear. I'm done having people protect me."

He heard what she didn't say. Her brother had protected her, and it had cost him his life.

"You can't blame yourself for what happened to your brother."

She shrugged. He wasn't going to change her mind and he knew it. He snorted. He also knew he was being a hypocrite. Wasn't he blaming himself for what had happened to Harrison, his old army buddy? Except he was at fault for that, at least partially. Unlike what had happened to Jacob.

Holding in a sigh, he pivoted on his heel in order to see what was left of the office. Not much, that was for sure. The barn next to where the office had been was unscathed.

"I don't know what your brother wanted you to find. Maybe, if we can get the tree moved, maybe we can search through all the debris and find something that will explain what's happening." He didn't hold out much hope, but they would never know until they searched.

She quirked an eyebrow. He recognized doubt when he saw it.

"*Jah*, I know we probably won't find anything. And, since you don't want to be lied to, I'm going to go out on a limb here and assume that whoever went through the trouble of sawing down that tree had already searched through the office. I'm guessing he didn't find what he was looking for and wanted to make sure no one else did, either."

Lilah chewed on her thumbnail. "Or he did find it but wanted to cover up the fact he'd been searching at all, so the police wouldn't come for him."

He considered that. It didn't ring true for him, but it was a possibility. *Jah*, a definite possibility. "Could be."

"So, do we still search?"

The bleakness lurking in those blue eyes blasted away at the wall around his heart. Her vulnerability was having a devastating effect on his mental state. He needed to change direction and focus on something other than Lilah Schwartz.

"I don't know we have any other choice."

He waited for her response. It wasn't long in coming. She pondered his statement for ten seconds or so before nodding her head.

"Assuming you're right, what's your suggestion?"

"Well, obviously we need to get rid of the tree." He removed his hat and wiped his brow with his sleeve. It was only a little after ten, but the heat was already sweltering. He sized up the tree. "We're going to need help. If I try to cut up the tree myself, we'll be here for days."

She glanced quickly at his right arm, then blushed, shifting. A thick, awkward silence fell between them. Levi had grown so used to his prosthetic arm, sometimes he forgot that others might not be as comfortable with it. He continued as if the awkward moment hadn't occurred.

"I'll see if my brothers can come and help us. Abram has a friend who runs a lumberyard. Maybe he can borrow a few tools. Saws and such. That should help us get the job done."

"I don't want to tell strangers what Jacob said."

"*Jah*, I get it. You don't want strangers to know that Jacob might have been in trouble." He rubbed his chin while he thought through their options. "Look, my brothers are at work anyway. They wouldn't be able to assist us until tomorrow morning, at the earliest. Let's go over and see if we can dig around the tree. Maybe we'll find something."

Lilah sighed, but didn't debate his statement. Together, they walked to the pile of splintered wood, branches and sawdust. She used her hands to pull up some of the smaller boards. Levi moved opposite her. He wasn't able to grab as much with his right arm, but he could get a hold on the smaller pieces. With his left, he lifted some heftier pieces. Under those pieces were more pieces. The stack of wood, debris and dust that had been her brother's office stood three feet high.

"Ouch!" Lilah jerked back, holding her left hand carefully. A large, jagged sliver was jammed into her flesh. Blood welled up around the projectile. A slow rivulet ran down the side of her hand.

"Oh, hey." He dropped the board he was holding and jogged around the pile to assist. Bracing her injured hand in his right, he used the left hand to gently pry the sliver loose. The cut was bleeding, but it wasn't deep. He rubbed the area with his finger to make sure he got the entire splinter out. A buzz of energy shot from her palm to his skin. He dropped her hand, the back of his neck heating up. He was acting like a teenager.

"It should be fine in a minute." He stepped back from her. "Does it hurt?"

Her eyes were wide. She'd felt it, too. Not *gut*. "*Nee*, not anymore."

He averted his gaze from the flush in her cheeks. "*Gut*. This is going to take a long time to dig through."

"Is it feasible?" Her sleeve brushed his arm as she moved up beside him. "I want to keep searching. The size of the woodpile is overwhelming, though."

That was putting it mildly.

"We have to try, *jah*?"

"We do." She threw him a shy smile. "I need to trust *Gott* more, I know. Sometimes it's hard."

Hard? He didn't want to admit how often he struggled with his faith. Oh, in his head, he believed, knew all the facts. But his heart, well, his heart had been closed for so long, he didn't know if it could open. He wasn't sure he wanted to discover if it was possible.

Maybe that was why his reactions to Lilah set him off-balance.

She was standing much too close. A warm breeze tickled his nostrils with the scent of lavender oil. He knew that smell. Among the Amish women who made their own soap, it was common to add in lavender oil. Lilah must have used the soap as shampoo. He caught himself in the act of inhaling to get a better whiff and clenched his teeth together. Where was his self-discipline? Distance. He needed distance between him and Lilah. However, it would be childish to move away again.

Levi had thought he was beyond being affected by the presence of a woman. None of the women his *mamm* had introduced him to had sparked any interest in him. And now, to find that he was as capable of being distracted by a pretty face as any man. Except Lilah wasn't just a pretty face. She had already shown tremendous courage, despite the blows she'd been dealt.

She was also a woman in danger.

"Here, help me lift that big board on the other side of the tree."

Lilah strode to the other end of the rough wooden plank. Some of the tension bled from his shoulders as the space between them grew wider, allowing him to breathe freely. Together, they heaved the large slab of wood and carried it sideways to a clear spot on the grass. There were so many trees in the area the grass was still damp with dew.

"*Danke*. Just a few more and we should be all set to go. Easy peasy."

He smiled as a discreet snicker met his ear. *Easy peasy* was a favorite phrase of one of his clients. He'd latched on to several phrases during his time as an *Englischer*. Sometimes, they slid out of his mouth before his brain could think of a better way to explain. Not that he would have tried that hard.

Lilah straightened, half turned, ready to go back for another board. The grass in front of her feet exploded. A familiar acrid odor rose in the air.

Gunpowder.

Someone was shooting at them.

"Get down!"

Levi leaped across the board, reaching Lilah as a second blast rent the air.

Heat and pain sizzled against his ribs.

He pulled her down in the grass, using his own body as a shield.

Please Gott, let me get her out of this. Alive.

Lilah hit the ground hard. The breath was knocked from her body. Before she could recover, she felt Levi slam into her. She cringed at the loud crack. A second bullet had been fired.

She didn't hear it hit anything.

For a moment, she imagined the shooter had missed his target. But something was wrong. It took her a second to realize what it was. Levi breathed in her ear, a harsh, rasping sound. She jostled him as she attempted to shift so his weight wasn't crushing her. He groaned. Lilah froze.

"Levi, are you hurt?"

He grunted. "I'll be fine. He nicked my side with that bullet."

She gasped. There wasn't enough air. Why wasn't there enough air? Lilah clenched her eyes shut, struggling to regain her composure. She couldn't panic. Not now.

But what was she supposed to do if Levi was injured? She couldn't leave him here and go get help, not with someone shooting at him. How would she even make it to the buggy? She'd be killed in the attempt. She didn't even consider trying to carry him to safety. Levi might not have been that tall, but he was all muscle. He had to outweigh her by fifty pounds. There was no way she would be able to drag him to safety.

"Calm down, Lilah." Levi's breath tickled

her ear as he spoke to her, his voice a low rumble. "There's no need to panic. I'll be fine. I won't leave you."

She frowned, irritated that he would make such an assumption about her.

"I'm not worried that you'll leave me," she hissed. "I'm worried that you'll get killed if I leave you."

She started with surprise when he chuckled. "My mistake. Stop talking. I need to listen."

Lilah nodded. She closed her eyes, trying to listen, as well. She couldn't hear anything out of the ordinary. Birdsong. The wind. A woodpecker was close by, hammering into a tree. All sounds she would have expected to hear.

What she didn't hear was more gunshots.

"Why did he stop shooting?" she risked asking. Hopefully, the shooter had gone, but she wasn't naïve enough to believe that.

"I don't know," he responded.

He was tense. She guessed Levi didn't like not knowing what the shooter was doing.

All talking ceased when a cell phone went off somewhere nearby. It was cut short abruptly. Branches rustled for a couple of seconds, breaking off and leaving a heavy, expectant silence.

"Amateur," Levi breathed, so low she had to

strain to hear him. Still, the disgust in his tone was clear. "I need you to trust me."

She wasn't going to like this. Her muscles tightened and her stomach clenched. Lilah nodded.

"I need you to crawl away from here. We need to get behind the barn. Follow me. Don't get up on your hands and knees. Keep low to the ground. Understand?"

Nausea flooded through her. She bit back a groan and forced herself to nod. *"Jah."*

Lilah wanted to ask why. She didn't, though. The back of the main barn was a few feet back from where the pile of debris extended. If the main door hadn't been blocked by the fallen tree, they could have gone into the barn and out the door on the other side.

And then her opportunity to ask any questions was gone. Levi was moving. The hiss he couldn't hold back as he eased away from her made her flinch. He was injured and in pain because of her. If she hadn't hidden in his barn, Levi would be safe at home.

Was she doomed to cause others harm?

She fought against the memories of Jacob's death. It would do no good to dwell on it now.

She needed to follow Levi's instructions. Only then could he get his injuries treated.

Lilah raised her head slightly and squinted as she followed Levi's progress with her eyes. He was mostly pulling himself along with his arms. She watched how his legs moved. He wasn't getting up on his knees.

After several failing attempts, Lilah started to edge her way behind the barn. Her ears strained for the crack of a gun going off. There was nothing. Sweat trickled on the back of her neck. Within minutes, her back was drenched. Her shoulder muscles ached from the abuse she was forcing them to go through.

And still she moved.

Levi was out of sight now. She had to keep going.

Inch by agonizing inch, she pulled herself across the wet grass. If she hadn't been wearing black, her dress would be ruined for sure. She would never get the grass stains out. But who cared about grass stains when they were a moment away from being murdered in cold blood?

The reminder of why she was crawling across the lawn reinvigorated her. With a sudden burst of speed, Lilah dragged herself behind the barn. Levi was waiting for her, his jaw tight. His obvious concern touched her.

Lilah arrived at his side. Levi grabbed her

hand and squeezed it. Before she could squeeze back, he released it and sank back against the ragged barn wood. Lilah opened her mouth, determined to ask Levi what his plan was. The thought froze in its tracks, her eyes wide as they fastened on the left side of Levi's blue shirt. A stain darkened it, continuing to spread.

He hadn't been nicked by a bullet.

He'd taken a direct shot. She knew about hunting. The bullet was possibly still in his side. He needed help, fast.

"Levi, a couple of inches, and he might have hit your heart."

"Nah—" he waved her concerns away "—I'm *gut*. You don't need to worry about me."

She was worried. His skin was pale, with a fine sheen of perspiration at his brow. He needed medical attention immediately. Unfortunately, they were stuck where they were while there was a man hunting them down.

Levi's eyes drifted shut.

"Hey, hey." Lilah fell to her knees beside him and patted his cheeks with her hands. "Levi, open your eyes. You can't sleep now. Please open them. Look at me. Levi!"

One eye popped open. "Why are you hitting me?"

She sat down on her heels, a sob clogging her throat. "I'm not hitting you. I'm trying to keep you conscious."

He sighed, his head fell back and his eyes closed again. "I appreciate the concern. I'm not falling asleep. I'm thinking."

"Well, think out loud," she snapped.

He huffed a short laugh. "I heard his phone go off. That's why I said he was an amateur. No one with training would have made such a rookie mistake."

She blinked. "What do you mean by that?"

Both eyes opened to peer at her. Pain radiated from them. But they were clear.

"I left the Amish for a time," Levi informed her. "In the years I was gone, I joined the military and served in Afghanistan."

She remembered him saying something about being away from the Amish. She'd been right about something else, too. He was a soldier. She held in her curiosity. Now was not the time.

"If our shooter had been trained, he would never have left his phone on. I'm glad he did, of course. It gave me his approximate position. I think once we went down, he was unable to see us behind the pile. Between the downed tree and the height of the destroyed shed, he couldn't see us as we crawled back here. Nor could he move without giving away his position."

She nodded. "*Gut*. So now what?"

"Now we make our escape and hope he hasn't found a way to leave his hiding spot."

FIVE

So far, so good.

Levi motioned for Lilah to stay close to the barn. She complied without question, turning her gaze upon him. The trust in her expression unnerved him. He squirmed under the weight of that gaze.

Since returning from Afghanistan, he'd lived a quiet life. One could almost say isolated. For a while, he'd even lived alone in a small *haus* he and his friend Aiden had built, surrounded by woods and security cameras. He was serious about his privacy and solitude. He hadn't put himself in situations where he was responsible for someone's safety and well-being to this extent.

Until now.

Not even when he was drawn into assisting Aiden to protect Sophie and her young sister Celine. Aiden had been the one in charge, the police officer guarding the woman being hunted. Levi had just been the sidekick. Oh, sure, he'd helped. He'd risked his life and even been injured. But he had never had the responsibility of making the decisions.

He'd avoided such situations on purpose. If he wasn't in charge, it was less likely that his decisions would cost anyone their life.

Not like it had been when he was soldier.

He brushed the memory aside like a bothersome cobweb. He was used to avoiding disturbing images from the past. Except while he slept. At night, those memories preyed upon him. It was rare that he enjoyed an uninterrupted rest.

His eyes settled on Lilah again. *Jah*, she was still gazing at him like he had all the answers. What would it be like to be worthy of such a woman? He snorted softly. What would she say if he told her he was winging it, as Aiden liked to say? He derived no pleasure from the conjecture. Her gaze burned through his barriers. The idea of disappointing her, or worse, of her being harmed through his failure, was unacceptable.

He had no choice. He would protect Lilah, and if he could, he would help her uncover what had happened to her brother and why. No matter the personal cost.

The burden settled uncomfortably on his shoulders.

His hand grazed his side. Pain pulsed through his side. He winced, then immediately straightened his features, hoping to disguise his reaction.

"You're in pain, aren't you?" Lilah hissed at him. Accusation rang in her tone, rather than the sympathy he would have expected. For some reason, that amused him. "Don't smile at me! You need to be tended to, soon!"

He kept his response low to avoid being overheard by the sniper hiding in the trees.

"*Ach*, Lilah, let's worry about getting out of this mess. You can scold me all you want later."

She flushed. Whether with shame or irritation, he wasn't sure. The glow looked better on her pretty face than its previous pallor.

"I'm not scolding. I'm concerned. You're still hurting, ain't so?"

"I'm fine. See?" He pulled his shirt gently away from his waist to give her a brief glance. "The bullet barely grazed me. It's stopped bleeding."

Her face wasn't merely pink. It was bright,

tomato red. He dropped his shirt down over the wound again.

He returned to the business at hand. "Listen, I think our sniper is actually up in the trees. Probably in the old tree stand that Jacob had set up to practice target shooting for deer season."

She scanned the trees. "I can't see it from here."

"*Jah*, it's not visible from here. If I'm right, then he can't see us. Nor will he be able to see us if we go through the trees, there." He pointed over to the side. "The problem is, once we reach the buggy, we'll be in plain view. So, you'll have to follow me close and try to step careful. We don't want to alert him to where we are heading."

"What if he leaves the tree stand?"

That was what he was concerned about.

"Honestly, I don't know. I have my doubts about his skills at stealth."

She frowned, her forehead creased.

"What I mean is I'm optimistic that he isn't used to this sort of thing." Maybe *optimistic* was too strong a word. He strongly hoped their sniper was a rookie, unused to the intricacies of stalking prey.

When she nodded, he blew out a breath and

motioned for her to follow him. "Stay low and do as I say without question."

Inching along the back of the barn, he arrived at the corner and squatted. Slowly, he peered around the corner, ready to duck behind cover instantly. He surveyed the area from the ground to the surrounding trees. Nothing suspicious popped out at him. Which didn't mean no threat was there.

Well, they couldn't stand here all day and wait for the shooter to come and get them.

"*Gott*, we could use some help." He prayed, casting a brief look up toward the sky.

Lilah exclaimed softly behind him. He hadn't meant the prayer to sound irreverent. It had been sincere. He could have prettied it up some, but he wasn't used to praying in front of others. And prayer was meant to be from the heart. To his way of thinking, nothing ruined a prayer more than making it conform to the preferences of other people. If you were saying it for their benefit, it wasn't truly communicating with *Gott*, was it?

"*Jah*, we could use lots of help," a soft voice echoed.

Her addition caught him by surprise. He chuckled and winked back at her.

Crouching low, he left the shelter of the

structure and made for the line of trees. Soft footsteps crunched behind him. *Gut.* Lilah was following. The safety of the trees had appeared close. Until one tried to get there, knowing there was a target on their back.

Sweat trickled down his forehead. Levi ignored it until it leaked into his eye. Wiping it away on his sleeve, he forged on. He kept his head up, constantly searching the trees and the landscape for any motion.

Hearing a noise off to his left, Levi motioned with his right hand for Lilah to stop.

She took one more step and stopped, so close he could have reached back and taken her hand.

He didn't, though his fingers twitched with the urge.

Motionless, they waited.

When nothing happened, he continued forward. She followed.

It took five minutes to reach the safety the line of large, elderly trees provided. There were majestic oaks, maples and even a few trees from the pine family. Their footsteps were muffled by the foliage resting on the floor. The branches and canopy provided cover. Had it been late fall or winter, they would have been in trouble.

Levi straightened, stretching his cramped back muscles. "We can move more freely here," he whispered. "But we still should stay as silent as we can."

Lilah took him at his word and nodded.

Leading the way, he continued walking. The goal was to get them back into the buggy. He wanted to make sure they came out of the woods slightly ahead of the buggy, about near the hindquarters of the mare. If all went as planned, the buggy would provide camouflage for them, keeping them from being seen by the sniper.

The tricky part would be getting up into the buggy without making any noise or without the horse fidgeting. Obviously, the moment the buggy started moving the shooter would know where they were. Levi was counting on the shooter needing a few minutes to get down from the tree stand in order to get to his vehicle to chase after them.

Of course, it was just as likely that the guy would just start taking shots at them from where he was. Their only option was they would have to stay low, and let the buggy take the brunt of the assault.

Just imagining putting Lilah in that kind of danger had him breaking out in a cold sweat.

He couldn't see any other way to do it, though. As much as he was pretending that his injury didn't hurt, he had lost some blood and didn't know if he would be able to walk all the way back to his parents' *haus*. Not to mention, sooner or later the sniper would discover they had escaped and would come searching for them. They couldn't stay in the woods forever. Walking on foot with no cover was out of the question. They had to have the buggy.

Turning to tell her the plan, he saw Lilah's foot hit a patch of mud. Her arms flailed as she slid. Jumping in front of her, he caught her as she pitched forward. Her arm struck out, banging into his injured side. For a moment, lights danced in front of his eyes. He wrapped his arms around her, taking her weight as she fell against him.

They wobbled for a few seconds. Levi's feet slid back.

Finally, he steadied them, and she found her feet.

He looked at her, ready to crack a joke, or make a light quip to ease the tension of the moment.

Instead, he found his glance landing on her lips. Smelled the lavender scent on her hair. Electricity sizzled in the air between them.

He dropped her arms and staggered away from her.

He would keep her safe. He would help her discover the truth. What he wouldn't do is allow this woman to destroy his peace of mind. Not because she was unworthy. *Nee*, Lilah Schwartz was completely worthy of a man's respect and devotion.

The problem was with him.

Lilah gave him a look filled with confusion and questions. She wasn't prepared for the attraction between them, either. Or maybe he had hurt her by his reaction to their closeness.

It was all for the best. If she really knew him, she'd understand that there was too much darkness in him.

But she'd never get that chance. Not if he could help it.

What had she done to cause that reaction from him?

One second, Levi caught her as she fell, the next he was practically tripping over himself to get away from her. It could have been embarrassment. Or his Amish sensibilities telling him it wasn't right to stand so with an unmarried *maidal*.

It wasn't. She knew his reaction had more to

do with the sparks dancing in the air around them. She'd felt it, too.

The experience wasn't pleasant. It rattled her. Hadn't she learned? Men were not trustworthy. At least not romantically. She didn't welcome the butterflies fluttering in her stomach when he got too close. She'd lost so much in her life. Risking her heart again was not something she was prepared to do.

She had to find out what happened to Jacob. Nothing else mattered, not until she accomplished that goal. It was the only way she could make reparation for all that she had cost him. His death had only been the last in a long line of sacrifices Jacob had borne out of love for his one sibling. Sacrifices that had come between him and Hannah and had lingered enough to poison her own relationship with her sister-in-law.

Levi was watching her, his eyes sharp and probing. She squirmed, her instinct to hide like an earthworm burrowed deep in the rich soil to escape the blistering heat of the sun.

"Where are we going, exactly? Are we purposely walking the boundaries of the property line?"

Levi had turned his back on her and started walking again. He answered over his shoulder.

"*Jah*. We couldn't walk directly to the buggy. We're going to walk to the front of it and hide behind it as we climb on."

A shiver worked its way across her shoulder blades. "He'll see us."

Levi halted and whirled to face her. In three steps he was at her side. His left hand lifted, then dropped back to his side. Had he planned on touching her, to reassure her?

"Lilah, I can't promise that we won't be seen."

"*Jah*. I know this. That's not something I'd expect of you."

He nodded his head toward where they'd come from. "I can't even promise that we won't get hurt. I will promise to do my best to get you out of here. And to keep you safe."

He glanced around. His sigh brushed against her cheeks like a caress. She blushed, then frowned, irritated with herself. It wasn't like her to be so silly about a man.

"If I were still *Englisch*, I would have owned my truck. We could have been gone already." He waggled his eyebrows at her. He gave a sigh rife with mock longing. "Four-wheel drive, you know."

She spluttered, half laughing, half shocked.

Satisfaction bloomed across his face. Ah, now she understood his strategy.

He wanted to distract her from her fears.

"Danke."

He nodded, confirming her suspicions. For all his prickles and defenses, Levi Burkholder was a *gut* man with a kind heart.

"All right, then. Let's go." She made her words firm. She was strong. And she was smart. If he told her to do something, she'd do her best to follow his instructions. If she didn't, both of them could pay for it.

With each step closer to the edge of the trees, Lilah's muscles tightened. Her heart raced so fast, soon it was hard to hear anything except for the blood pumping in her ears. Her stomach was crunched into a hard ball by the time she stepped up beside Levi.

His narrow stare scanned the yard. His blank expression chilled her. This was not the same man who had bemoaned not having his four-wheel drive truck. *Nee*, this was a man who had gone to war and seen violence. Possibly, he'd killed for his country. She couldn't imagine what that kind of experience would do to one's soul.

The buggy was exactly where they'd left it.

The mare still standing placidly, grazing on the grass on the side of the drive.

"I'll go first. If no one shoots at me, follow."

Levi lifted a leg to walk to the buggy.

"Wait!" She grabbed his arm, panicked. "What do I do if you are shot?"

He froze for a moment before placing his left hand over hers. "If I'm shot, I want you to run."

She started shaking her head and backed away. Crossing her arms over her chest, she glared at him. "I will not leave you here to be killed! What a horrible idea!"

"Lilah, you have to." He placed a finger under her chin and applied enough pressure to bring her eyes up to meet his. "If you don't run, we're both dead. If I get shot, you will be my only hope. Go, find help. Call the police, an ambulance. Whatever we need. You will be the only one who can."

She didn't like it, but she nodded her agreement. There was a community phone booth less than a mile from their position. She'd never needed to use it before. She held her breath as Levi turned away from her.

He crouched and edged out into the open, soundlessly creeping across the open space that stretched out between the buggy and the safety of her hiding place.

She hated this plan.

He arrived at the buggy, carefully easing himself up inside the black boxlike vehicle, staying low. Once he was inside, she relaxed. If the shooter didn't look through the tiny rear window, all would be well.

Until they started moving.

It was her turn. Lilah mimicked Levi's approach. Her legs were trembling so hard each movement felt like she was trying to walk a thin tightrope. She lost all sense of time. It could have been minutes or an hour. When she joined Levi at the buggy, he hauled her inside.

For a moment, her nose was buried in his chest as he hugged her. She felt him trembling. For all his calm expression, she knew the truth. Watching her walk across that short expanse of open driveway had terrified him.

Then she was free. He made no mention of what had occurred. In fact, he didn't speak at all. Both hands moved out and caught the reins.

Neither of them was sitting fully on the seat yet. As he settled back, the mare nickered and pranced, jostling the buggy. Levi's shoulder slammed against the wall of the buggy. It swayed.

For one horrified moment, they froze, eyes clashing in disbelief.

Glancing back to where her brother had his tree stand, she gasped.

A man was scrambling out, a rifle in his hand.

Levi exploded up and sat firmly on the seat. Clenching the reins, he flicked them, sending the mare into a canter.

A bullet cracked and slammed into the back of the buggy with a clang.

Another flick of the reins. The mare sped up, careening out onto the road. The buggy swayed and swerved dangerously.

Lilah started praying. They had maybe a minute, maybe one and a half, before the man from the tree stand made it to his car and came after them, intent on taking their lives.

SIX

Lilah started to rise. Levi barked at her to stay down. Freezing at his harsh command, she remained on the floor of the buggy, leg muscles cramping painfully. Riding sideways in such an uncomfortable position, she understood what seasickness must feel like. Her stomach began to roil. She lowered her head and closed her eyes.

When she started feeling light-headed, she couldn't take it anymore. Lilah heaved herself up and slid onto the seat. She expected Levi to rebuke her. He didn't, though his mouth tightened. She must have looked as ill as she felt.

Then she noticed the strain around his eyes. His complexion was gray.

She glanced down at his side. The stain was spreading. He'd reopened his wound.

"Levi, you're bleeding again." Her voice rose.

"Jah," he grunted. His breathing was harsh. "I bumped it when the mare bolted."

He was close to passing out. Lilah reached out and grabbed the reins from him.

"Hey—" His normally robust voice was thin.

"You're going to pass out at any moment." Her glance darted around. "We have to get off the road. He'll be by any moment. We can't outrun him."

Seeing a dirt road on the right, Lilah made a split-second decision and steered the mare down the road. It was little more than a tractor path. Spying an opening in the trees, she used the reins to direct the mare off the road and toward the opening.

The buggy was snug in its little alcove.

Lilah watched the road they'd come from, anxiously. A minute later, she heard the roar of an engine a second before a green Jeep, covered with dirt and dust, sailed by. She didn't have a clear view of the driver, but she was positive it was the shooter. She clearly recalled a green Jeep passing the Burkholder *haus* the day she'd arrived there. Was that only two days ago?

"We can't stay here for long," Levi murmured.

"*Jah*, I know. I just want to wait a few more

minutes. I have a feeling he'll *cumme* back this way."

Levi groaned and attempted to straighten from the slouch he'd fallen into. She placed her hand against his shoulder. Gave it a slight push.

"Stop. Rest for a few minutes. If we don't see anything, we'll go."

Five minutes later, the green Jeep passed again, going back toward what was left of her *haus*. She waited another moment, then urged the mare out of its hiding spot.

"Let's go back to my *haus*," Levi suggested. "I can get patched up, and we can plan our next move."

She didn't like it. It felt too much like giving up. But what other choice was open to them? She had a feeling the sniper was heading back to her place.

"I wonder if he's waiting for backup to help him search."

"Could be. Or maybe we surprised him before he had a chance to leave this morning. Funny, I hadn't noticed the Jeep on the property."

She shrugged. "I didn't either, but that doesn't surprise me. You must have noticed how the weeds had grown up on the west side of the *haus*. We stopped mowing that section years ago. It would've been easy to hide a vehicle in there. Actually, you could have hidden several cars there, and I never would have noticed."

He chuckled. She frowned at how tired it sounded. Levi was so intense, his current condition was all the more striking. It was like finding a tiger and hearing it meow. Unexpected and disconcerting. She hoped it wasn't too serious. Maybe he'd be fine after the wound was cleaned and he had time to rest.

She peered over at Levi again, half-afraid he'd drifted off. He'd become quiet in the past few minutes. Too quiet. She didn't have any medical training, but she knew more than she'd ever wanted to know about injuries and blood loss. The accident that had taken her parents and left her in Jacob's care five years ago was not something she was likely to forget, no matter how many years *Gott* planned for her to live on Earth.

She needed to shake this mood she was in. A dark cloud of gloom and weariness hung over her, dragging her spirits down. She was more exhausted than she had thought, and no wonder. The past few days had been one harrowing event after another. The worst of course had been when Jacob had died. But then she'd been kicked out of her temporary home, been shot at, and now the man who rescued her and was trying to assist her had been injured on her account.

By the time Lilah steered the horse and buggy into Levi's driveway, tears were building behind her eyelids. She sniffed and clenched her teeth together, willing them away. Crying wasn't going to help her.

She halted the buggy in front of the porch. It should probably go back into the barn, but she needed to get Levi inside.

His mother made her way painfully to the porch. *Nee.* She wasn't going to tax that sweet woman any more than was absolutely necessary.

"Levi." Smiling at his mother, she jostled him awake.

"*Jah.* I'm awake."

"*Gut.* Your *mamm* is waiting for us. You should put on a smile and prove you can walk on your own, ain't so?"

He sat up, his posture stiff. Agony radiated off him. But he didn't complain.

"I can help, if you need me to," she offered but wasn't surprised when he refused.

"*Nee.* I can do it." A glimmer of humor appeared in his eyes. He spoke out of the corner of his mouth, his lips barely moving. "You're right. *Mamm* will be less concerned if I walk into the *haus* independently."

She tore her gaze from him, flushing. She'd been entranced by his impromptu ventriloquist display. So entranced that she'd been staring at his mouth. Ducking her head, she sped up in an effort to hide her face from him. She had to fight this attraction between them.

His chuckle vibrated along her nerves. He knew what she was doing, she was sure of it.

She joined Fannie on the porch. Levi's mother smiled at her, but her gaze sharpened as it zeroed in on the splotch darkening his shirt.

"Levi? What's wrong? *Bist du verletzt?*" Fannie demanded.

Levi waved his hand, but the gesture appeared stiff to Lilah. He was in pain, but she knew he wouldn't admit it. Not because of macho pride. *Nee*, Levi didn't want his *mamm* to be anxious. Which was ridiculous. Mothers always worried when their *kinder* were injured or scared.

"It's fine, *Mamm*." He mounted the steps slowly. "A small injury. I just need to clean it."

Fannie Burkholder wasn't having it. She planted her fists firmly on her hips and stood in his path. Eyes wide, Levi had no choice but to stop. It was either that or skirt around his mother.

"You are hurt, and you will let me tend your wound." Fannie's voice was soft as velvet, but steel rang just below the surface.

Lilah heard it. The expression on his face told her Levi had heard and recognized it, too.

Shifting to the side, Lilah waited until they had moved past her before following them inside the *haus*. She was numb. Levi would be fine if he hadn't been helping her. How long would it take until Fannie came to the same conclusion?

She'd already been kicked out of one *haus*. Would the Burkholders make her leave, too?

She had nowhere else to hide.

His *mamm* could have been a drill sergeant.

People often saw her as frail. In some ways, she was. The arthritis had taken its toll on her for the past few years. The moment she started talking, though, he knew better than to argue. He'd heard that particular tone often enough to know any "discussion" would be fruitless. His *mamm* was bone stubborn when she chose to be.

Now was one of those times.

Holding in a sigh, he allowed himself to be prodded and scolded as she cleaned and dressed his wound. He'd been right. It had ached, and would be sore for a while yet, but the bullet had merely grazed him. He'd had worse.

Much worse.

He flexed the fingers of his right arm. The movement wasn't as precise as his left, and it was limited. But he had more than many of the guys he'd served with had.

"Levi?" His *mamm* had finished and was frowning at him, furrows lining her face under its simple prayer *kapp*.

He stopped messing around and dropped his right arm, uneasy. He was grateful for the prosthetic limb. It was a blessing he hadn't expected from an unexpected source. But he also didn't like calling attention to it.

Where was Lilah?

He'd been so deep in his thoughts, he'd not been aware of the movement around him. He scanned the room for the pretty blonde, finally finding her hovering right inside the kitchen doorway. She hadn't come very far into the *haus*.

Her posture reminded him of how she'd appeared when he'd found her huddled up in his barn. He took in the rounded shoulders, the arms crossed over her middle as if to hold herself together and the weary droop to her mouth. As his gaze clashed with hers, her posture tightened further. The anxious cast to her face was wiped clean, leaving it smooth and without expression.

Her whole demeanor told him she expected to be tossed out on her ear.

Like what had happened to her with her sister-in-law.

Not happening.

"Lilah."

She flinched at his voice, overloud in the still room. He softened it. "Sorry. Didn't mean to shout."

She didn't respond.

He tried again.

"Lilah, my getting shot?" His *mamm* gasped at this piece of information, which was not helpful. He squeezed his mother's arm but kept his glance firmly on Lilah. "This isn't your fault."

She lowered her gaze and stared at the floor. "Isn't it?"

He could barely hear her.

"Please look at me." He waited until she did so. "You didn't ask for any of this to happen.

Whatever your brother got himself involved with, that's on him."

He was unprepared for her strangled sob that hit him like a fist to the chest. She dragged in a deep breath, fighting for control.

His mother gathered up the bandage supplies she'd used on his side and slipped from the room. The quiet enveloped them. He let it settle around them, affecting a calm he didn't feel.

"It feels like it's my fault," she muttered.

He huffed. He'd started to think she'd never respond.

She edged closer to where he sat at the kitchen table, halting a couple of feet from where he sat. He wished she'd sit. It was awkward craning his neck to look up at her. Of course, he could fix that by standing. He was too done in to move, though.

"Why would it be your fault?" Maybe logic would work.

"I'm his sister. Until you asked me if I'd noticed any changes in him, I hadn't realized that Jacob had changed. Shouldn't I have? We lived in the same house. I saw him every day."

Levi tilted his head to the side, considering his next words. "I think that was probably the crux of the problem, right?"

Twin furrows streaked across her forehead. "Explain that."

She walked over to the table and lowered herself into a chair. Levi twisted around so he was facing her direction.

"It's simple. We don't always notice people changing when we see them daily. But I'm sure if you were to go and visit a friend or a cousin you hadn't seen in a long time, your first thought would be how different they'd become."

Her lips ticked up at the corners. Not a full smile, but close.

"*Jah.* That is so. That would explain why Hannah never seemed to notice a difference, either. But you would just expect a wife to notice, wouldn't you?"

"Not necessarily. Jacob might have been good at hiding it. Plus, I would imagine lots of things were changing in her life. It's possible she was too distracted herself to notice any differences in her husband's behavior. You know, with a *boppli* on the way. Especially the first."

He grinned at the tide of red flowing up her cheeks. Obviously, Lilah's family didn't discuss such things. It was the way many Amish districts handled such a delicate subject. It wasn't unusual for parents not to say anything to older *kinder* until their *mamm* had the *boppli* in her arms. He'd been out in the *Englisch* world long enough that such matters no longer made him squirm.

He shifted gears.

"Anyway, we're not going to make you leave. You can stay here as long as it takes to find the truth."

Tears puddled in her eyes, but she blinked them back.

"*Danke*. I have nowhere else to go."

"No problem. I think we'll have to alter our plan, though."

She sat forward in her seat. "Oh? How?"

Tension crept into her tone.

"*Jah*. I'm sorry, Lilah. If someone is out there waiting with a gun, I don't want to risk asking my brothers to come help without getting the police involved."

She hesitated. "I don't know—"

"We can't do this alone. Think about it. These guys, whoever was after your brother and is now chasing you, they aren't done."

"You're right."

The words were dragged from her. Well, he didn't need her to like the plan. Just to accept it.

As a rule, the Amish were reluctant to go

to the police for assistance. The current situation, however, was one time he'd make an exception. Lilah and he had both been shot at on two separate ventures to get into her brother's office. Coupled with the trouble someone had taken to destroy the evidence, Levi was convinced the danger was only beginning.

If they weren't careful, this could end badly, with someone else getting hurt.

Or dying.

He wouldn't let that happen to Lilah. Levi refused to consider why protecting her was so important. He had been a soldier. Protecting people, fighting for them, had been part of his reason for getting up in the morning.

It was different with her.

He shoved the thought aside. He wasn't getting involved with anyone, not even a spunky blonde who made his heartbeat quicken, not ever. And especially not when they were literally involved in a small battle to gather answers and get out alive.

SEVEN

Never in her wildest dreams had Lilah ever imagined that she would need to go to the *Englisch* police for anything. Her brother hadn't even sued the driver who had been responsible for their parents' deaths and their medical needs years ago. And those weren't the only bad things that had happened in the past. On the contrary, she could think of several instances it might have been nice to have had outside support. Say, when someone broke into Jacob's office two years ago...

She gasped as a new possibility popped into her mind. A very unwelcome possibility.

"What? What's wrong?"

Levi grabbed her hand where it rested on the table. She tugged. He held on. In fact, his grip tightened. Looking at his face, she didn't think he was even aware of it. Alarm dug deep creases in his forehead and deepened the downward curve of his lips.

Letting her hand lie beneath his for a moment, she forced her thoughts away from the warmth oozing into her skin.

"I remembered something. I can't believe I never connected it before..." She shook her head, snorting a bit in her disgust. She hadn't been very observant.

"Lilah, what?" Amusement warred with impatience in his tone. At least some of the tension had drained away. Still, her heart ached at the weariness lining his eyes and mouth.

What was she thinking? Until a few days ago, she had never met this man. She was more rattled than she'd thought. She needed to move her hand. If she did, though, it might look like she was overreacting to what was surely a supportive gesture.

He was still waiting for her response.

"About two years ago, shortly before Jacob married Hannah, his office was broken into. Nothing was stolen, or that was what he said. I'm not sure I believe that anymore. I guess I forgot about it, but now, I wonder if it's all connected to what has happened in the past week."

"Could be." Levi nodded, removing his hand from hers to run it through his hair. She missed the feeling of his hand touching hers, which wasn't a good sign. Lilah clasped her hands together to be sure he didn't put his back on hers. "To be honest, I'd say it almost definitely is connected. It's too much of a coincidence not to be. Someone definitely wants something your brother was hiding."

She nodded, not liking where this was going. "I think they would have stopped searching if they'd found it."

"Maybe so, maybe not. We won't know until we get more information. Speculation won't give us the answers we need."

Lilah stood to wander the room, needing space to think. "We can't wait until tomorrow. I hate the thought of losing any more time."

"Agreed." Levi stood, stretching. He winced and placed a hand over his side. "Ouch. Shouldn't have done that."

She bit back an inquiry about how he was feeling. Even if his side hurt, he wasn't letting it hold him back. She'd respect his privacy. If he wanted to tell her how his side was faring, he would.

He wandered over to the window and placed his left hand high against the frame. Leaning in, his keen glance scoured the yard outside.

"It's not that late. Let's grab a quick lunch, then we can head into town."

Lilah gnawed on her bottom lip. "Um. Just a thought… Should we maybe hire a driver?"

"Short notice for a driver, ain't so?"

"*Jah*, but do we really want to be driving a buggy to the police station when someone is after us with a gun? Levi, he's shot at me and he's hit you. He knows what we look like. If it's someone from around here, he might even know who you are."

"You could be right. I'll go to the barn and see if I can find a driver. We might need to wait until tomorrow, though."

She frowned. She didn't want to wait. Not because she was impatient, although she was. "I hope not. If we have to wait, then that gives them, whoever 'them' is, more time to find whatever they were looking for."

"*Jah.* But if they found it, maybe they'd leave you alone."

She thanked him with a scowl. "If it was bad enough to kill for, I doubt it would stop them. Besides, for all he knows, we may have seen the man who shot us. We did see his car."

"Are you waiting here while I call around?"

"*Nee*, absolutely not."

He sighed. "I didn't think you would."

He grabbed his hat and left the *haus*, clunking down the steps in his heavy work boots. It hit her as funny, but she squelched her giggles.

"What are you carrying on about back there?"

She did her best to control her giggles, but a muffled snort slipped out. She slapped her hand over her mouth, appalled that she'd done that in front of him.

He covered his mouth and coughed.

Narrowing her eyes, she glared at him. That cough sounded a lot like a snicker.

"Seriously, Lilah, what's so funny?"

Shrugging her shoulders, she sent him an apologetic smile. "Sorry. I didn't mean to laugh. It just struck me as funny. Normally you walk so quiet, literally soundless. Until you hit your mother's stairs and then you sound like a rhino tripping down the steps."

"What, really? A rhino? I've never heard myself compared to a rhino before. Kind of ugly critters."

She sniffed. "All *Gott*'s creatures are beautiful."

They reached the barn. She followed him inside, blinking as her sight adjusted to entering the dim structure after being outside in the bright sunlight. She stopped so as not to fall over anything. Thirty seconds later, her vision acclimated to the new surroundings, she hurried to catch up to Levi.

He was already on the phone, calling the first number. No answer. The second number picked up, but they were already booked. The third number, the person was available tomorrow morning at the earliest.

By the time he was dialing the fourth number, she was discouraged. She still didn't feel it would be smart to take a buggy out again. But neither did she want to wait. It looked like they might have to. She chewed on her thumbnail, listening as Levi started talking to the fourth driver.

She pulled her hand away from her mouth when his eyes flared wide-open.

"*Jah?* You are available in two hours?" Levi looked at her. "*Jah*, we will be ready. *Danke!*"

He finalized the details, then hung up. "Okay, Owen, our driver, will be here in two hours. I've never hired him before, but he has *gut* references. Let's go eat and then we can plan our strategy. What we'll tell the police."

She nearly had to run to keep up with him on the way back to the *haus*. They were really doing it. They were really going to involve the *Englisch* police.

Hannah wouldn't be happy.

Hannah.

Lilah came to a full stop, her brain screeching out an alarm.

"Levi!"

He spun. Surprise flared on his face when he saw her standing still in the middle of the driveway.

"Lilah?" He marched back to where she stood. "Why are you standing here?"

"Levi, what are we going to tell the police about Hannah?"

His eyebrows arched. "About Hannah? Why should we tell them anything about your sister-in-law?"

"Because she knew about the arson and didn't mention it to me. Remember? I still think that's suspicious. Don't you?"

He waved it away. "Maybe. I don't know. She's been under a lot of stress, *jah*? Emotionally, and even physically."

She knew he was referring to her condition. Thankfully, he didn't dwell on it.

"So?"

"So, I think we should give her some grace. People act funny when they are going through stress or emotional times." His expression darkened. "Trust me, Lilah. I have seen this personally. I would not want to be judged on my own state of mind during such times."

It made sense, what he was saying. But what if he were wrong?

"How about this," she suggested. "We will go past the Hostetler *haus* on the way to the police station. Could we stop by and talk with Hannah? For five minutes?"

Levi sighed.

"I won't pressure her. I will try not to upset her. I just want to know, in her own words, what the fire chief told her."

"Then you can compare it to what we learn at the police station, *jah*?"

She nodded, playing with her kapp strings.

"Smart," he announced. "You won't accuse her of anything, but will find out if she lied to you or deliberately misled you."

"Exactly." She wasn't used to be underhanded. However, considering the circumstances, she didn't feel bad about it.

To her surprise, he went along with the plan. They went inside and ate some of his mother's amazing cooking. Lilah loved to cook and bake. When she was at home and felt sad, she baked cookies or brownies. Jacob had always loved sweets. Hannah, although a wonderful *gut* cook, disliked baking. She was more than happy to let Lilah handle that chore.

Crunching into Fannie's nut and chocolate chip cookies, Lilah hummed in pleasure. She itched to get her hands on the recipe.

"You like them?"

She nodded at the older woman, her mouth still full of the chocolaty goodness. Swallowing, she took a drink of water to wash it down. "*Jah*, the cookies are *gut*! Exactly what I needed."

Before more could be said, a vehicle pulled into the gravel driveway and sat idling.

"Time to go."

Levi stood and jammed his hat on his head. Lilah thanked his mother and strode out with him to the car.

"You Owen?" Levi asked.

"At your service," a jovial voice answered. "You must be Levi."

"*Jah*." Levi opened the back door for Lilah and let her in before climbing in the front seat next to Owen. She was only too happy not to be sitting up next to a stranger, even one as friendly as Owen. The accident that had taken her parents had also taken two years of her life, leaving her somewhat shy.

It was amazing how comfortable she was around Levi.

It couldn't last, of course. It never did. Something always happened to rip away her joy and tear her down.

Levi chatted idly with Owen as they headed toward the Hostetler place. Owen was amusing, his comments and stories had a sardonic wit that normally would have made Levi chuckle. Today, though, he had difficulty focusing on the conversation. Instead, his mind kept revisiting the conversation he had with Lilah earlier.

He knew her idea to go and see Hannah before they went to the police station had merit, but he still wasn't completely sold on the idea. Hannah had already hurt her, although he didn't blame her. Not really. He hadn't been kidding when he said people who were hurting, mentally, physically or emotionally, could react out of character to stressful situations. He remembered his own days in Afghanistan. He especially remembered the weeks following Harrison's death. He had not been himself, that was clear. Thankfully, he wasn't alone. Even when he was in the wounded warrior hospital, there were counselors and other vets who understood his state of mind. The depression and the anger that waged war inside him. He felt a shudder working its way through him and forced it back. He didn't ever want to deal with a tragedy or emotional devastation like that again.

Thankfully, Aiden had found him again after he returned to the States. That was what had really saved him. Aiden, the best friend he'd ever had, standing by his side and keeping him from doing anything really stupid.

Aiden helping him through those first days when he'd grow frustrated at trying to work with his new arm. Aiden was also the one who had come up with the idea of building something to take his mind off his troubles and to prove to him that he could do it. He'd lived in that *haus* for a time.

He shook his head. Now was not the time to think about that episode in his life. Even though it was one that would affect the rest of his life.

He was so caught up in his memories, he nearly missed that Owen was nearing the Hostetler *haus*.

"Okay, Owen. The next driveway on the right will be it." He sat forward, scanning the area to see if there was anything suspicious.

Nothing struck him as off. He still couldn't shake the sense that something was wrong.

"Got it." Owen slowed down and put on his blinker, even though no one was coming the other direction. Levi approved. You never knew when someone would come flying up from behind.

Owen turned right into the driveway leading to Hannah's parents' *haus*. He parked at the side of the *haus*. The Hostetlers had a small area off to the left of the driveway where cars could pull in and easily turn around. Owen backed into the space.

"We shouldn't be too long," Levi told him.

"I'll wait. Doesn't matter to me how long it takes. I have nothing else going on today. Might even catch a short nap while you're gone."

Levi thanked the man, then pulled on the handle and swung the door open. He climbed out and opened the back door. Waiting for Lilah to meet him on the driveway, he scanned the area again.

Funny. Middle of the day, and there was no movement. Plus, it was laundry day. There were no clothes hanging on the line. Odd. Stretching his neck slightly, he peered at the *haus* across the street, which was owned by another Amish family. Sure enough, sheets waved at him from the clothesline.

"Where's the laundry?" Lilah murmured, echoing his thoughts. "I know Hannah's *mamm*. She'd have been on the third load of clothes by now."

Something wasn't right.

"Maybe she's ill." He didn't believe it, though.

"Even so, Hannah is here, and she is *gut* and strong. She would make sure the laundry was done."

"What about the other *kinder*?" He knew so little about the Hostetler family.

"Hannah is the youngest girl. Her five sisters all have families of their own. Her oldest brother lives here. He's at work during the day, and his *frau* cleans *hauser* for *Englischers*. They wouldn't be home now."

But Hannah and her parents should be.

"Lilah, could you go sit in the car?" He didn't want her to be anywhere near the *haus* if his instincts were right.

She didn't want to, opened her mouth, presumably to argue, then shut it again. "I don't want to," she whispered, casting a sideways glance at the *haus*, "but I know if something is wrong, then I'll be in your way."

He nodded, grateful for her understanding.

"Be quick," she ordered before scurrying to the car. He could see her talking to Owen but turned away. It didn't matter what she told the driver. She was safer in the car than in the *haus*.

Levi placed his foot on the first step as if it were covered with eggshells that he didn't want to crack open. There were four steps. The third step creaked. He froze but didn't hear anything.

Advancing to the door, he saw that the main door was wide-open, and only the flimsiest of screen doors barred him from the interior of the *haus*. It wasn't even latched all the way closed.

Grabbing the door, he inched it open just wide enough to fit his frame through. Easing inside, he paused to listen for any sounds coming from within the *haus*.

Nothing.

He left the kitchen and ventured through the wide arching doorframe into the front room.

He stopped three feet inside the doorway.

He had found Hannah's parents.

They were lying side by side on the floor in the middle of the room, both so still his heart stopped for a moment. He didn't need to move closer to know that the small puddle on the floor next to Frau Hostetler was blood.

Levi looked down at his hands. The room wavered briefly. He sank back against the doorway. Squeezing his eyes shut, machine gun fire blasted in his mind. He slapped his hands over his ears. It was no good. He could still hear it, the sound vibrated in his bones, careening through his soul. He panted. He needed to leave. Had to find Harrison and Jones. They should have been back by now. His eyes returned to the prone bodies on the floor. Soldiers. There were soldiers all around him.

Harrison. Lifeless eyes staring back at him. He had no idea what had hit him. The ambush had taken them completely by surprise. None of them had had time to react. His rifle had been heavy in his hands. Useless. No one was left.

Where was Jones?

Levi looked around the front room, but he saw none of it.

His mind was clenched in the grasp of the horrors only people could perpetrate on each other.

Levi spun in a wide circle, seeing the chaos and devastation around him. His arm swept something over. It crashed. His vision was blurry, clouded with smoke. He couldn't see what it was.

He could call for help. Maybe the enemy was still lurking. If he called, they'd know someone was left. They'd come back for him.

Aiden. His buddy had been with him when they'd found the bodies.

Where was he? Had he been caught, possibly killed?

Levi shook, his teeth chattering inside his mouth.

He had to get away from here. Spinning on his heel, he ran into something. It was hard and heavy and in his way. Shoving out his arms, he pushed the object away. When it tipped over, the explosion forced him to his knees.

Levi pushed his hands against the floor, fighting to remain conscious. Acrid smoke filled his nostrils. Gunfire spat around him.

He was lost.

EIGHT

What was that sound? It was like something had crashed and shattered. Something heavy. And was that Levi yelling inside the haus? Was he calling for her?

Nee, that was a scream of anguish.

"I'll be back!" she hollered to Owen as she thrust open the car door.

"I'm comin' with you," he responded. "He sounds like he needs help."

Running around the car, they pounded up the stairs and burst into the *haus*. The yelling had stopped. All she heard was someone breathing harshly in the next room. Levi.

Lilah ran into the room, then stopped abruptly. Owen slammed into her and she fell forward. She caught herself before she fell.

Her eyes fell on the couple lying on the floor. Hannah's parents. The color drained from her face. Hannah's *mamm* was moaning. At least she was alive. She wasn't sure about her *daed* yet.

A soft moan had her whirling to the right. Levi was sitting on the ground, his arms around his head. What was wrong with him?

"He's having a flashback," Owen murmured behind her.

"A what?"

Owen squatted down in front of Levi. "Was he a soldier or something?"

She hesitated, then nodded. It wasn't her secret, but if it would allow her to help Levi, she would tell Owen. He seemed to have guessed anyway.

"Lots of them came back suffering from horribly intense memories of what they saw. I recognize the signs. I have a cousin who has flashbacks. I'm guessing seeing those people on the floor was a trigger. It pushed him mentally back to the war he was in. You stay here with him. I'm going to see what I can do for those folks and call 911."

She nodded to show she understood, but never removed her gaze from Levi. She had no experience with anything like this. Was it like sleepwalking? She'd heard one should never wake a person when that happened.

"Owen, can I talk to him?" Owen seemed

to know more than she did. "Try to pull him out of it?"

"I don't see why not," he answered, crouched between Ben and Waneta. "They're both alive. Knocked 'em on their heads pretty good."

He whipped out his cell phone and tapped the keys. He began speaking almost at once. She tuned out his low voice as he talked with the dispatcher at the 911 center.

Lilah returned her focus to Levi. "Hi, Levi. Can you hear me?"

No response.

She reached out and touched his arm. When that didn't do anything, she wrapped gentle fingers around his wrist.

His head snapped up. Lilah's breath got stuck in her throat at the agony on his face. She didn't move. There was a wildness in his gaze that told her he wasn't completely with her yet. She didn't want to take a chance on doing more harm. She couldn't imagine the terrifying memories he must have.

After a few moments, the wildness faded from his face. He pulled his arm away from her. His face closed off. Cautiously, he surveyed the scene. When his attention landed on the Amish couple lying on the floor, his entire face tightened. His jaw worked back and forth. He was grinding his teeth.

"Levi," she breathed, *"bist du gut?"*

She cringed after the ridiculous question left her mouth. Obviously, he wasn't well. If he'd been well, she wouldn't be sitting three feet away from him, afraid of saying the wrong thing.

"Jah," he rasped. "I'm fine. Just give me a moment, will you?"

She backed away, stunned by the sense of rejection his words caused. He hadn't meant it that way, most likely, but that's how it felt.

The feeling was becoming far too familiar. Lilah was done with people closing her out. Hannah had done it. Her brother hadn't shut her out, but he'd clearly been lying to her, which was just as bad. And now Levi.

But he's in pain.

She sighed and let the bitterness go. Levi had been brave and selfless for the past two days. He'd taken on her cause and had been injured in the process. She couldn't turn on him when he needed her to give him space.

The ambulance arrived, splashing red strobe lights against the walls. Lilah went to the door to let the EMTs in. A second ambulance pulled in as they were going through to the other room.

She led the second pair of EMTs through.

"Hey, Mickey. What do we have?" The man behind her edged around her and went to kneel by the one he'd called Mickey.

"Hiya, Calvin. It looks like both of them were struck in the back of the head. Female patient, altered level of consciousness."

Lilah peered at Mrs. Hostetler. She was awake but didn't appear to be aware of them. After a few seconds, her lids closed.

Mickey continued. "Male patient, still unconscious. Vital signs…"

The next minute was filled with technical jargon Lilah didn't understand.

She left them and headed back toward Levi. She halted when a third vehicle pulled in, lights flashing. This time a police car. They were completely hemmed in by emergency vehicles.

She went to find Owen. He was sitting in the kitchen, away from all the noise. Levi was poised near the window. He caught her eye briefly when she joined them. His mouth tipped up at the corners, short of a true smile, but close enough that some of the knots in her stomach dissolved. He'd be *gut*.

Owen was playing on his phone. It was beeping and buzzing at an alarming rate. "Hey,

Lilah. We're keeping out of their way until they need us. Have a seat."

"Owen," she whispered. "Why are the police here?"

He looked up from his phone. "Standard procedure. When you call 911 and report that two people have been attacked and need an ambulance, the dispatcher will automatically notify the law, as well. I know Plain folk don't typically go to the police, but this was one time it couldn't be helped."

"I'm not faulting you," she hurried to say. "I didn't understand, is all."

Owen shrugged his meaty shoulders and smiled. "No offense taken."

She opened her mouth to say more but paused when hard shoes clomped on the hardwood floor behind them. Turning, she found herself staring into a face not much older than her own. The young woman in the police uniform marched into the room with an air of confidence that Lilah admired.

"Afternoon," she greeted Lilah, Levi and Owen. "My name's Officer Nicole Dawson. I have a few questions about what happened here, if you don't mind."

Lilah allowed herself a small smile as amusement wove its way into her mind. Whether they minded or not, she had no doubt Officer Dawson would take their statements. If the matter weren't so serious, she might have been tempted to try out her theory, although of course she never would. That would be disrespectful, and Lilah tried to always treat others with respect.

Levi's glance meshed with hers. He was smiling, too. She had the sense that they were thinking along the same lines.

"*Nee*, we don't mind," she answered the officer.

"Good. Now, you called it in." She pointed to Owen. "I understand you are often hired to drive Amish people places?"

"Yes, ma'am." He ducked his head. "That's what I was doing this afternoon."

"Why don't we start with why you came here and what you found."

Levi cleared his throat. When Lilah glanced his way, he had turned and was facing them, hands behind his back, legs slightly spread.

"We were coming here to see Hannah Hostetler. She's Lilah's sister-in-law." He jerked his chin in Lilah's direction. "Hannah's husband Jacob, who was also Lilah's brother, was killed in a fire nearly a week ago. When we arrived, I found Hannah's parents on the floor as you saw them when you entered. I have not seen Hannah."

"I noticed some items were destroyed. The small curio cabinet had been knocked over."

He paused, a shade of uneasiness crossing his face.

Suddenly, Lilah remembered hearing a crash. The cabinet hadn't been knocked over by the person who'd attacked the elderly couple. It had been a victim of Levi's flashback.

Well, the police didn't need to know he suffered like that. It had no bearing on what had happened to the Hostetlers or Hannah.

"Sorry. We knocked that over when we saw what had happened. It was an accident."

The woman narrowed her eyes at Lilah. Suspicion tainted her expression.

"It's okay, Lilah," Levi said. He met Officer Dawson's stare with one of his own. "I was in Afghanistan some years back. When I saw Hannah's parents, I had a flashback. Knocked the curio cabinet over without realizing what I was doing."

The suspicion melted away. Compassion and understanding replaced it.

"Thank you for your service," the officer told him. "Sorry you had to deal with this."

She turned to Lilah, which was good, because she could see Levi was squirming at her words. He wasn't one who enjoyed talking about himself to strangers.

"I'm sorry about your brother, Lilah. What can you tell me about Hannah?"

She flushed. "Well, she's twenty-one years old. Has dark blond hair and greenish-brown eyes, and she's seven and a half months pregnant."

The officer's spine straightened and her expression grew grim. "Do you have any reason to believe she may have been involved in what happened to her parents? Could she have run away with, ah, a boyfriend?"

Lilah's mouth dropped open. "*Nee!* Hannah loved my brother. She wouldn't do that to him. Never!"

The officer asked a few more questions. By the time she walked into the next room, Lilah's ire had started to ease. Her stomach roiled at the mere suggestion of such behavior. Hannah may not have been receptive to her after Jacob's death, but she knew that the other girl would have never betrayed him.

Officer Dawson returned a few minutes later and leveled a flat stare at Levi and Lilah.

"One more question. Did you know the fire that destroyed your house and killed your brother was arson?"

* * *

Levi stiffened, his gaze zeroing in on Lilah. She blanched, but other than that showed no reaction. He clenched his left hand into a fist. If he had his druthers, he'd go and sit down next to her, letting her know he was there to support her.

He didn't, though. Levi stayed near the window, standing in his at ease stance. Lilah was strong. While he didn't know everything in her past, he knew enough to know that she had survived her share of traumatic events. She didn't need him to save her.

Even if that was the one thing his instincts were screaming at him to do.

"When was the last time you saw Hannah Hostetler?" Officer Dawson inquired.

"Schwartz." Lilah's voice was soft as she corrected the officer. "My sister-in-law's name is Hannah Schwartz."

Officer Dawson frowned. "Excuse me. When was the last time you saw Hannah?"

Lilah chewed on her fingernail briefly. Levi had seen her do that enough to know that she was either nervous or deep in thought. Possibly both, considering the circumstances.

"The last time I saw Hannah was two days

ago, on Saturday. That was the day of my brother's funeral."

"Thank you. Did anything appear to be bothering her at the time?"

Lilah's eyebrows climbed up her forehead at the ridiculous question. "Um. *Jah*. Her husband was dead and her home was gone."

An unfamiliar sarcasm dripped from her words.

"And she was expecting," Levi murmured.

"*Jah*, she was expecting their first *boppli*, and knew she'd be raising her *kind* without a father."

"Fair enough." The officer jotted down a note in her notebook. "Anything beyond that?"

Lilah's blue eyes blazed with indignation and her pale cheeks flushed with temper. She was getting very close to the end of what she could tolerate. Levi said a quick prayer that she could hold on.

"*Jah*, something else was bothering her. She was angry with me because if my brother had not needed to go back into the *haus* to save me, he wouldn't have died that night."

Her questions might have been intrusive, but Levi believed the police officer had a good heart and was just doing her job. Although, he winced at the inherent insensitivity of the questions.

"Miss Schwartz, I apologize for upsetting you. I promise, my only intention is to find the truth. Sometimes, that means I have to ask tough questions."

Levi couldn't take it anymore. He stalked to the table and pushed a chair next to Lilah before dropping down in it. He didn't touch her. He didn't need to. The grateful look she sent his way told him she understood.

Didn't mean he didn't want to touch her. *Jah*, he wished he could reach out and grab her hand to comfort her. He wasn't sure she'd let him. He'd upset her earlier, and although she'd apparently decided not to hold a grudge, he could sense a new distance between them.

The officer started to rise. Levi exchanged a glance with Lilah. It wasn't the way they'd planned it, but they'd still set out to go to the police. He raised one brow, asking permission. She nodded.

"Actually, Officer Dawson, we have something we wanted to talk with you about before you leave." He slid a glance to Owen. "It's private."

Owen's mouth gaped for a second. "Oh! I guess I'll go out to my car. You all come out when you're ready for a ride back to your place."

They waited until the door closed behind Owen and his footsteps had clomped down the wooden stairs.

"Okay, what did you want to talk with me about?" Officer Dawson asked, curiosity sitting openly on her face.

"We were coming into town to go to the police today," Lilah began. She stopped and looked at Levi.

This time he did grab her hand. When she didn't protest, he hung on. "Lilah had gone to her brother's office after the funeral on Saturday. Someone was in it and had chased her and shot at her. When we went there this morning, someone was shooting at us, sniper style."

"Levi got hit." Lilah's whisper caught him off guard. He found himself snagged by the vulnerable light in her glance.

Shaking himself free, he returned his attention to Officer Dawson. "A graze. Nothing serious. I don't need to go to the hospital."

Her sharp glance pinned them. "I need to see where you were shot."

Flushing, he pulled his shirt up just enough to show the bandage. Using his right hand, he maneuvered the bionic fingers to grip and pull the bandage to show the wound.

"Do you have any idea why someone would want into your brother's office?"

Lilah nodded slowly. "Maybe so. I think he had something in there, something hidden that could get someone in trouble. Right before he died, he told me to go to his office and find something. He died before he could tell me where to look or what I would be searching for."

"We were going to search this morning, but we couldn't even get into the office," Levi continued. He told the officer about the tree that had smashed into the office, and how he suspected it had been cut down deliberately.

"Probably to keep others from getting suspicious," she mused.

"*Jah*, that's what Levi and I thought," Lilah informed her.

This time when Officer Dawson rose, they rose with her. "You can't go back to the office now," she said. Lilah opened her mouth, but the officer cut her off. "It's going to be a crime scene. We'll search, and let you know if we find anything."

She turned away, before turning back. "Oh,

two more questions. You said the sniper chased you. What kind of vehicle?"

"It was a dark green Jeep," Levi responded. "We didn't get a license plate number. I'm pretty sure there was too much dirt to see it, even if we'd thought to look. Nor did we really see the guy."

She grimaced. Levi was thankful she wasn't asking them to come in to look at mug shots. It would be pointless, and he wanted to be done for the day. He still couldn't get the images of Hannah's parents lying in their own blood out of his head.

"Last question. Lilah, if Hannah was your sister-in-law, why weren't you staying here?"

Lilah's head fell forward. Levi could almost feel the grief swelling up inside her. Yet, when she lifted her head, he couldn't see any tears. He knew they had to be simmering beneath the surface.

"I wasn't living here because Hannah asked me to leave after the funeral. She didn't want me around after what had happened to Jacob."

"Hmm."

Levi narrowed his stare at her. "You think Hannah's involved."

"I'm not saying anything. Remember, don't

go to the office until you get the all clear from me. I'll be in touch."

The moment she was gone, Lilah rounded on him. "What makes you sure she thinks Hannah's involved?"

He rubbed his neck. "I would. Hannah kicks you out. Maybe to get you out of the way. Your brother's office is targeted. If she was working with someone, wouldn't she know that he'd likely hide something there? As you mentioned before, she didn't tell you about the arson. Then we arrive, her parents are hurt, but not dead, and she's gone. No sign of struggle."

She was already shaking her head. "I don't care how much sense it makes, I won't believe it."

"Well, believe it or not, she's who the cops are looking at first."

"She didn't do it, Levi. She had survived something truly tragic. That's why she asked me to leave."

His hand landed softly on her shoulder. "I believe you, Lilah. But I think the police will need more proof than that."

She moved away from him, and his hand dropped back to his side. "Does this mean that they will not look for the man in the green Jeep?"

"*Nee.* They can search for both."

She bit her lip again. Seriously, he found that habit of hers distracting. He already liked too much about her. He was not a good candidate for a husband, which meant he couldn't get emotionally entangled. Or let a woman get emotionally attached to him.

A hollowness in the pit of his stomach told him it might be too late, at least for him.

Lilah opened the door and stepped out onto the steps. She started down them but when she got to the bottom, she turned to face Levi. Whatever she was planning to say vanished when her eyes widened and she pointed at the railing.

Levi hurried down and looked at where she pointed.

On the railing of the Hostetler's immaculately kept *haus*, where every inch of the *haus* and porch looked freshly painted, there was a splotch, the shape of a human palm.

It was blood.

NINE

Whose blood was it?

A hollow pit in his gut told him it was Hannah's. Despite all the circumstantial evidence to the contrary, Levi trusted Lilah's take on her sister-in-law. Fragile, overwhelmed and scared. She was not a cold-blooded killer.

But someone was. Someone who felt the need to get rid of Jacob and his family, and Levi, due to his connection with Lilah.

Levi could probably end the threat to himself by removing himself from Lilah's life. He wanted to be able to live with himself, though. He couldn't walk away, not now that he knew his friend had been murdered. And not after seeing for himself that an innocent woman was being put in harm's way. She wouldn't give up the search for answers, so until answers were found, she would continue to be in mortal danger.

Levi opened the back door and waited while Lilah climbed in. Her face was chalk white, her lips pale and pinched at the corners. She didn't speak. He gently shut the door behind her and opened the front door. He sank down onto the seat beside Owen's.

Twisting in his seat, he moved so he had a clear view of Lilah. She was staring out the window. The strain of the past few days was stamped on her face. She sagged back against the seat, defeated.

"Hey," he called to her softly.

She dragged her eyes from the window, one eyebrow quirked in a question.

"We're not giving up. We'll find Hannah. And…" He remembered Owen sitting next to him. No need to give an outsider more information than necessary. "We'll keep searching for the other thing, too."

Her lips tilted up. She shot a discreet glance toward the driver, nodding. She understood his message. They could have switched to Pennsylvania Dutch. For many Amish families, the unique dialect with German roots was the main language spoken at home. It would have been rude, however, to isolate Owen that way.

"I have been selfish."

Lilah's words startled him.

"Why would you say that?" Levi slid a glance toward Owen. The man could hear them, but he didn't appear interested in their conversation. Still, it wasn't exactly ideal to have anyone listening in.

She shrugged, leaning her head against the window. "You've gone through so much for me. And your family, too. I hate that my problems are going to continue to intrude on your life."

"Not for long. But it doesn't matter."

He dropped the subject since they had an audience.

A few minutes later, Owen whistled. Levi's head jerked up. Lilah groaned.

They were driving past her *haus*. There was already a police cruiser sitting in the driveway.

"Wow, that place is a mess," Owen remarked.

His cheerful voice grated on Levi's nerves. It bordered on rude and was inappropriate, in his opinion. It was also cruel, which surprised him. Owen had been there when the police were talking about the fire. Had he not put two and two together and realized this was Lilah's *haus*? He didn't dare look back at Lilah. He didn't want to draw Owen's eyes to her and expose her pain.

Levi changed the subject and began chatting about the events happening in Berlin for the next few weeks. Tourism was booming and Owen jumped into the conversation enthusiastically, completely dropping the topic of Lilah's *haus*.

"*Jah.* I drive a buggy for the Amish Country Tours." The business was actually in Sutter Springs and not Berlin. But it was close enough that he could drive into Berlin and visit some of the Amish run shops and businesses if that was what the clients wanted to see. "They sell out nearly every day. We have to turn walk-ins away. Most of them *cumme* back," Levi mentioned. That was far more personal information than he usually gave anyone, but he wanted to give Lilah time to regain her composure if she needed it.

He wilted back against his seat when Owen pulled into his driveway. He was a *gut* driver and Levi appreciated his being available on such short notice, but he was a bit nosy. And over-the-top cheerful.

Although, that probably said more about Levi than it did Owen.

Good humor restored, he paid the driver and opened the back door for Lilah. She slid out and brushed past him, leaving a trace of lavender scent in her wake. He shut the door and watched her mount the stairs and enter his *haus*, before turning in time to see Owen's car disappear in the same direction they'd recently come from.

Lilah exited the *haus* as he made his way over, two glasses of lemonade in her hands. He gratefully took one and sank down on the top step, waving for her to join him.

She smoothed her skirt down and lowered herself to the step, keeping a good two feet of open space between them. He noted the careful way she settled herself. The large distance was no accident.

He took a small sip of the cold lemonade, then a larger gulp. It was *gut*.

"Levi."

He glanced over. Her eyes fell before his. Her hands wrapped around her glass.

"Jah?"

She opened her mouth. Closed it. Started again. "What happened to you? At Hannah's *haus*?"

His hand jerked and he spilled lemonade on the lower step. She started to get up, but he motioned her back.

"Leave it."

"I shouldn't have asked," she apologized.

"I don't like to talk about it, but you had to deal with it. So, I guess maybe you have a right to know. If the sniper had been there, you would have been in danger. So, I'm sorry."

He took another drink to settle his thoughts. "You know I left the Amish for a few years, ain't so?"

She nodded but didn't say anything.

"I left after arguing with *Daed*. I didn't plan on ever coming back. I met a guy, Aiden Forster, and he and I got to be *gut* friends. The best. When Aiden told me he was enlisting, I thought, why not? It's not normal, but we were deployed together. Along with some other guys. One of them, Harrison, started to hang out with us. He was this great big guy, with a big voice and an even bigger heart."

Thinking about Harrison, he turned his head so she wouldn't see the pain on his face. He swallowed the lump lodged in his throat.

"Levi—"

"I'm okay," he croaked out. "Give me a minute."

He breathed in deep to get himself under control. "We were going out on a surveillance mission. I was supposed to go with Harrison, and we were meeting another team. But I got careless and the Major held me back to yell at me. Harrison went with Jones, another guy in our unit." He slammed his eyes shut, twisting his head away as if he could block out what was coming.

"They were ambushed. All six of the men on the mission were killed before they even knew what was happening. Aiden and I got there too late to stop it. The enemy were still shooting. Everywhere I looked, I saw fire and smoke. I went a little crazy, I guess. I couldn't leave without Harrison. He was dead, I knew that, but I dragged his body out. When my arm was hit, I was forced to drag him one-handed."

He stopped, unable to go on for a minute.

The scent of lavender reached him, soothing him. He opened his eyes. She'd scooted closer to him. Her hand reached out to rest on his left hand.

"I'm so sorry about your friend."

"*Jah*. Me, too. He'd saved my life less than a month before. Pushed me out of the way of falling boulders. Getting shot as I pulled him out was the end of the army for me. I lost my arm from the elbow down. Harrison's parents were all kinds of thankful I'd rescued his body. They had something to bury, and that was important to them. After my arm healed, I found out that they were paying all my medical bills, all of them. They even paid for my prosthetic arm."

He held up the hand and flexed the silver

fingers. "Fancy, ain't it? It's called a LUKE. Which stands for Life Under Kinetic Evolution. I don't really understand what that means, only that I can pick up a glass or simple tools with it. It's not capable of everything my arm could do, but it does more than I ever expected."

She looked at the arm, frowning. "It looks closer to a flesh arm than I would have expected, except of course for the color."

He shifted, thinking that might be enough. He caught her glance. *Nee*, she wanted more.

"You want to know about the flashbacks."

For a moment, Lilah felt mean.

Then she stiffened her shoulders. He'd known what she wanted to know. She linked her hands together on her knees and waited.

He sat back on the step and stared straight out in front. "I have what's called PTSD. Post-traumatic stress disorder. It's fairly common for soldiers. Or anyone who's been under trauma. Sometimes I have nightmares. Like nights where the thunder is loud, I can't sleep."

"You're afraid to close your eyes," she murmured.

He jerked his head toward her. "How did you know?"

She settled her chin on her clasped hands. "After the accident that killed my parents, I had nightmares for the first two years. Sometimes I still have them, though not as violently. Maybe because I spent all my time learning to walk again."

"Learning to walk?" He sounded horrified. She felt bad about the conversation switching to be about her, but maybe it was *gut*. If he learned about her flaws and issues, perhaps he'd feel less vulnerable telling her about his.

"*Jah*. The entire left side of the van we were in was destroyed. It's amazing I survived at all. My left leg was broken in two places. I was in a full leg cast for two months. After not using my leg for so long, the muscles had gotten weak. I needed physical therapy to build them back to strength. It took months."

He nodded. "*Jah*, I can understand that. It took a long time to learn how to use this arm, too."

They both stopped talking when his mother came to the door, asking if they wanted more lemonade. They both declined, then waited while she walked slowly back into the *haus*. He stood, glancing back at where his mother had been.

"Let's walk."

She followed, aware he wouldn't want his

mother to hear how he had suffered, and in fact, was still suffering, from his time in the military.

They wandered away from the *haus* and out beyond the barn. The Burkholder family kept a robust vegetable garden. Levi picked up a wooden crate.

"My brother Sam left this out here. We can gather some vegetables while we talk." They started with the tomato plants, selecting ripe Roma tomatoes, bright orange red in color, and carefully placing them into the crate. As they moved on to the broccoli, Levi talked.

"I haven't had a flashback for over a year. I had begun to believe I was free of them. But seeing those poor people, lying there in their own blood…"

He shook his head. "One minute I was in the Hostetler *haus*, the next I was in Afghanistan, searching for my unit. Seeing their bodies. I could hear them scream, smell the desert air and the fumes of the fire. I knocked over that curio cabinet without being aware I did it."

She remembered. "I heard the crash, then you started yelling."

"I think that's when I thought there was an explosion around me." He dropped an eggplant in the crate and lifted his gaze to meet hers. "I heard your voice and it pulled me out. I thought

I was getting better. Maybe I'll never be better. Sometimes it feels like *Gott* is punishing me for leaving home."

She didn't think, just acted. Her hand was on his cheek, feeling the slight bristle of his late-afternoon whiskers. His eyes widened, startled. He didn't pull back. Neither did she. All the words of comfort she'd meant to say dried up inside her mouth.

She wanted him to kiss her.

The thought shocked her out of the daze brought on by the connection. She jerked her hand away as if it had been burned.

"Sorry! I shouldn't have touched you. Oh, how mortifying."

His chuckle hit her ears and she glared. She didn't think there was anything funny about it.

He gestured to the garden around them. "I never thought of lettuce as romantic before, but hey, what do I know."

A giggle popped out of her mouth. She slapped her hand over her lips. It was relief, she knew, but it broke some of the tension growing in the air between them. They completed collecting the vegetables, then headed back to the *haus*.

"I don't think you're looking at this the right way," she said.

"What do you mean?" They paused on the driveway.

"You said you thought *Gott* was punishing you. That was why you had the flashback today. But you also said they're getting better. And today, I was able to bring you out of it. So, it seems to me *Gott* is right there beside you, giving you strength."

He thought about it. "Maybe so. Let's go in. It's almost time for supper. *Daed* will be home soon."

They cleaned up and joined his family for dinner. They sat at the table, and each member bowed their head to pray silently until David lifted his head to indicate prayer time was concluded.

Fannie had cooked a delicious and filling dinner. Lilah hadn't felt hungry until the aroma of fresh dumplings tickled her nose. Her stomach grumbled loudly, causing her to flush.

"I heard something today." Sam wiped his mouth on a napkin before addressing Lilah again. "Someone at the lumberyard was saying that Ben and Waneta Hostetler were attacked in their home, and their daughter Hannah was missing. Ain't that your family, Lilah?"

Lilah's cup hit the table and bounced, splashing water on her plate and on her dress.

Levi shot to his feet and grabbed the towel sitting on the counter. He handed it to Lilah. She wiped off the table. Her dinner was ruined.

"Do you need a new plate?" Levi was already reaching into the cupboard.

"*Nee*, I was finished." She hadn't been, but the reminder of what had happened had the food she'd already eaten sitting like a brick in her stomach. There was no way she'd be able to continue eating now.

A stifled silence filled the room. She looked across the table. Poor Sam. He looked pretty miserable.

"To answer your question, Ben and Waneta are Hannah's *mamm* and *daed*. I don't think of them as family, but they've been very kind to me. Hannah is missing, and the *Englisch* police are investigating. That's all I can tell you."

Sam peeked at her under his shaggy blond bangs. "Sorry. Didn't mean to make you feel bad. I was curious and didn't stop to think."

"Don't worry about it."

What else was she to say? He was nineteen, old enough to know better, but he hadn't been trying to upset anyone.

When the meal was over, the men all rose to head outside to help David for a few minutes. Levi pressed his hand on her shoulder for a second. When she met his concerned glance, she gave him a tired smile. It had been a brutal day. All she wanted was to go to sleep to get several hours' respite from the fear and uncertainty. But she wasn't going to tell him that. He had disrupted his life for her.

He searched her face before squeezing her shoulder slightly and marching out after his siblings and father.

Lilah remained in the *haus* and assisted Fannie with cleaning the dishes and putting the kitchen in order. She tried her best, but had trouble keeping track of the conversation. Fannie gave her a sympathetic smile and let her work in peace.

Lilah felt bad, but her head felt like it was ready to explode. She didn't ask Fannie for any painkillers for her headache. She didn't like to rely on medication. She remembered too well the feeling of the strong narcotics the doctors had given her after her parents had died. The medicine had made her feel like she was wrapped in a cocoon. All she had wanted to do was snuggle into it and sleep.

It was a *gut* feeling. And a dangerous one.

She hadn't told Jacob why she refused to take any more of her prescription. After two days of feeling like she was drifting, she'd been wary of taking any more. Lilah had decided to use over-the-counter medicines or live with the pain. She had shied away from relying on medicine since.

Telling Fannie she needed to lie down, she headed toward the stairs. Her feet were like blocks of lead.

Her tiredness vanished in a rush of adrenaline when she looked out the front window and saw a police cruiser pulling into the driveway. Her heartbeat ramped up. Ditching her plan to go rest, she pivoted and ran to the back door. She pushed it open and stood on the porch as the car stopped beside the *haus*.

Tapping her foot, Lilah waited while the engine shut off and Officer Nicole Dawson pushed the door open and stood.

When the officer's eyes met hers, Lilah clasped her hands together in front of her.

Her headache forgotten, she waited, the food she'd eaten an uncomfortable lump in her belly.

She knew why the officer was here.

They'd found something. And she had no idea if it was *gut* or bad. Only one way to find out.

She went down the steps to meet the officer.

TEN

Levi heard a car pull in and excused himself. Leaving his brothers, he strode from the barn. When he saw Officer Dawson chatting with Lilah, he stretched his legs to quicken his pace until he reached them. They broke off their conversation as he approached and waited for him to join them.

"Levi." Officer Dawson acknowledged him. "How's the side?"

"Better. *Danke*. You have news." It came out as a statement. Obviously, she had something to tell them or she wouldn't have come.

A glimmer of humor sparked in her eyes.

"Okay, so let's get straight to the point." The humor drained. The shift from chatty to cop was uncanny. "After I left the Hostetler place this afternoon, I took a drive to your property, Lilah."

She couldn't very well say *haus*, Levi thought ironically.

"*Jah*, we saw a police car in the drive as went past," Lilah informed her. "I was amazed that the police had arrived so fast."

"Yeah, well, both your place and the Hostetler property were set up as crime scenes within an hour. We found nothing more at the Hostetlers'—"

"What about the handprint on the railing?" Lilah blurted.

Levi nodded. "We were wondering if that could have been Hannah's. I figured you must have seen it. Otherwise, I would have told you about it."

Given the location, there was no way a trained police officer would have missed it. Especially considering that the elderly couple had been attacked.

"I am still looking into who the handprint belongs to. It may have been Hannah's. Or someone else involved. We do know it didn't belong to the man we picked up at your place, Lilah."

"What man?" Levi and Lilah both demanded, their words tumbling over each other. This was the first he'd heard of them arresting anyone at Lilah's place. Was it the sniper?

"Do either of you recognize this man?" Officer Dawson drew her cell phone from her back pocket, unlocked it and brought up a picture to show them.

Leaning in, he looked at the familiar image, feeling sick to his stomach. Lilah exclaimed beside him.

"Is that Billy?" she asked. "Levi, is that the man we met this morning?"

Officer Dawson answered for him. "That is William Whitman. He's got a record, misdemeanors mainly. We found him digging around inside your barn, Miss Schwartz. He hasn't told us what he was looking for. Since he has requested a lawyer, there's nothing else we can do at the moment. I was hoping one of you could shed some light on why he might have been at your place. Any ideas?"

Levi shook his head, then turned and cocked an eyebrow at Lilah. She looked as confused as he felt. She shook her head and grimaced in response to his unspoken question.

"I only met him for the first time today. He seemed to be a very friendly sort of person, except when he thought we weren't watching he glared at me. It was a very angry, almost hateful look. I have no idea what could've caused that."

"He had known your brother." Now, why had he brought that up? "I didn't mean that the way it sounded," Levi said.

While Officer Dawson seemed intrigued by his statement, Lilah paled as if he had struck her. He knew what she was worried about. Lilah was concerned that anyone looking into the situation might think Jacob had done something wrong. The idea had been on both of their minds. It was clear that Jacob had gotten himself into something.

Levi held up his hands. "I just meant that maybe Billy Whitman's presence could have been innocent. Maybe he was looking for something that Jacob had borrowed."

Even he didn't believe his words.

"What can you tell me about him?" The police officer had her notepad out and her pen ready to write.

Levi scratched his chin, searching through his memories. "Not that much. I have a car of his that I'm working on. I do mechanic jobs on the side. I've known him for several years, but we've never really talked about anything except for cars. I know his parents are divorced, and he grew up in Indiana. But that's about it."

"I'd love to dig around his car, but unfortunately I can't do that without getting a search warrant for it. I might be back. If I can get one, do you have any problem with me coming and looking through his vehicle?"

Levi shook his head. "I'm working on several cars, so let me show you which one is his."

She agreed rapidly. Levi led her back to the car. It was an old convertible, and Billy had kept it in pristine condition.

"Wow, this certainly is a beauty." Officer Dawson clasped her hands behind her back and took a leisurely stroll around the car. "Nice. It would be a shame to have to search through this. Sometimes things can get damaged in a search. He obviously took very good care of this thing."

"I do recall him saying that he took it around to different car shows. He's very proud of it."

She finished her inspection and turned back to them. "I'm hoping that if we tell him were getting a search warrant to search his car, then maybe Billy will decide to talk to us and save his car. I would sure hate to be the one to scratch the paint on something this well taken care of."

It was just a car. Sometimes the lure of possessions was scary. After he had left, he had been initially fascinated with the outside world. When he came back to the United States, that fascination had almost completely died out. After dealing with the trauma of seeing so many people injured and killed, the race to own more possessions, to build up more wealth completely left him cold.

"I'm sorry I couldn't shed more light on what he was doing when you found him," Levi said.

Lilah still hadn't said anything more. She seemed preoccupied. Levi wondered briefly if she was even paying attention to the conversation that was going on right in front of her.

"Well, whatever he was doing, we'll do our best to find out." The police officer stepped back a couple of paces, preparing to return to her car. "I just thought you should know what our search turned up. We found nothing else. Nothing that we could detect would lead to someone murdering your brother. The place is no longer a crime scene. I wanted to let you know personally."

No longer a crime scene. That meant they could enter the property. The police might not have found anything, but they weren't familiar with the layout of the land. Lilah was. He sneaked a peek at her. Her usually open face was blank. Whatever she was thinking, she was keeping it to herself.

Not that he blamed her. Letting outsiders know what was going on in their world never came easy. He just hoped she wasn't going to shut him out after his blunder about Billy knowing Jacob.

He knew she wouldn't ask him to lie to the police. It wasn't that. The crux of the problem was that she didn't know what Jacob had gotten into. Maybe if they had that information, it would be easier for them to figure out what to do next.

Which meant they had to keep digging for the truth.

They stood together on the driveway as the officer left. Levi edged closer to Lilah. "Hey. Are you okay?"

She startled. "Oh! *Jah.* I'm *gut.* I'm worried about Hannah. What if Billy took her? If the police have him, she might be somewhere all alone."

He thought about that for a moment. "True. But, if he's the one who hurt her parents, then she's probably better off by herself than if he were with her." He grimaced. "I don't know, Lilah. It doesn't feel right to me."

"What?" She glanced up at him. "What doesn't feel right?"

Without thinking, he reached out and took

her hand. The moment he did, they both froze. Now what should he do? He tugged at her hand and started walking. As they walked side by side, he dropped her hand. He couldn't resist giving it a light squeeze before he did so. Now, what had she asked?

"I have trouble seeing Billy as a kidnapper. I definitely can't see him as a sniper."

"But you do think he was involved." Lilah wasn't asking.

"I do. At the very least, I think he knows something about what has been going on. I keep remembering the look on his face when we saw him earlier. Nothing about that look makes sense. That wasn't the guy I knew. So now I'm questioning if everything I knew about Billy was an act. Again, that doesn't make sense."

For a moment, silence fell between them. It was a companionable silence. Despite the drama of the past two days, Lilah was a restful companion.

If only he were free to enjoy her presence. But the death of her brother and the missing Hannah loomed over him. There would be no peace until the truth was revealed.

His soul shuddered at the thought. Because once this case was solved and the villains were locked up, Lilah would go back to her life, and Levi would remain here.

The life he had been content to lead only two days earlier now stretched out bleak and empty before him.

Something was bothering Levi, but Lilah had no idea what. Or rather, which of the many things wrong it could be. Her brother's death, she was now certain, had been murder. Had the killer just wanted Jacob dead, or had Hannah been a target as well?

Hannah's abduction seemed to point to her being the target.

Lilah recalled Jacob's final words. *Nee.* He had definitely been part of it, too. What had they been hiding from her? And how long had it been going on?

Shaking off the gloomy past, she slanted a glance back at Levi. He still seemed somber. His thoughts were obviously dark, as dark as hers had been.

A thought occurred to her.

"Levi?"

"Jah?"

"If my *haus* is no longer a crime scene, and if Billy's in jail, maybe we could go over and search again. I know there's something there.

Something that Jacob wanted me to find. If the police found Billy but didn't find anything on him, maybe whatever Jacob had hidden is still there."

He frowned, pondering what she had said.

"I'm not so sure that would be a good idea," he began slowly. "If I'm right and Billy isn't the sniper, that means whoever was shooting at us is still out there."

"It was just a thought." Frustration bit at her, but there was nothing she could do. She wasn't going to go back there by herself. It just didn't seem to make sense. But she knew there was something there. Something that would explain everything that had happened.

She had to know.

Even if it wasn't a good idea, she started to think that maybe she should go back and search alone. It was, after all, her problem. She had dragged Levi into it. But it wasn't his responsibility. Jacob had been her brother, not his.

"You're planning on going back, aren't you?"

Startled, Lilah jerked her head up. Levi stepped closer, so close his breath hit her face in little puffs. She could smell mint and coffee. Realizing she was leaning forward, she backed up, her cheeks blazing.

She cleared her throat to regain her composure, noting that Levi was looking a bit flustered, too. Evidently, she wasn't the only one feeling the attraction. She had no intention of giving in. Until she found out what happened to her brother, nothing else mattered.

Unfortunately, all the clues were leading toward her brother having lied to her. She had trusted him implicitly. She trusted Levi, too, despite her intention to keep her distance. That wasn't a good thing. People you trust sometimes betray you.

"I have to keep searching. We're close... I feel it. And until I know everything, I don't know if I'll ever be able to sleep soundly again. I'll always be worried that someone is coming after me."

A sigh burst from him. "Fine. I get it. This time, let's leave the buggy in an area that won't be so obvious. Then if we need to escape, we could have a route planned out."

That sounded like a good idea.

"We'll leave early in the morning. Okay?" Levi lowered his chin to look her straight in the eye.

The pulse at her throat beat wildly at the

intense glance, but she resisted its pull. "That sounds fine. Will your mother mind if we help ourselves to breakfast instead of eating with the family?"

"It shouldn't be a problem. I'll ask Samuel if he can take care of my chores in the morning." He lifted his left hand and touched her cheek with two fingers. The tenderness of the caress had her catching her breath. "I will do everything I can to help you find the truth. You know that, right?"

She nodded. She knew it, but would it be enough?

That night Lilah lay in bed, tossing and turning. She was exhausted, so tired she felt like her limbs were weighted down. Yet still sleep eluded her. Thoughts chased each other inside her head. If she could just turn off her mind. No matter how hard she tried to clear her head, each and every time she closed her eyes, she would see Ben and Waneta Hostetler. In the early hours of the morning she finally drifted off. But the nightmares that chased after her left her groggy and even more exhausted than she'd been when she'd gone to bed the night before.

Finally, she gave up. Tossing back the sheet

she used as a light covering, Lilah padded on bare feet across the room to the window. The cold floor against the soles of her feet helped to wake her up so that by the time she reached the window, her grogginess had faded.

All she needed was a good cup of coffee and she would be up for the rest of the day. It was still dark out, although she could see streaks of lighter sky on the horizon. As she watched, the ink black sky gave way to streaks of orange and yellow and red, and even some pink.

A tear tracked down her cheek. She would have loved to have been able to share this vision with Jacob. That would never happen again.

Oddly, she also wished Levi were here to share it with her.

Nonsense. Making as little noise as possible, she got ready for the day. Once she was as clean and presentable as she could make herself, and her blond hair was neatly rebraided and stuffed beneath her prayer *kapp*, she slipped out of her bedroom door, holding her boots in her hand, and went on whisper-soft steps to the kitchen.

Levi was already awake, a fresh pot of coffee brewing. When he turned and saw her, he got her a mug and poured her some of the hot liquid.

She put in a small dose of cream and added a teaspoon of sugar before drinking.

"We should be going if we're going to do this."

She knew Levi was giving her one last chance to back out if she wanted to. She couldn't. Not yet. She couldn't back out and maybe never learn what had happened.

He read her expression.

"Okay. Let's go."

Levi already had the buggy hitched and ready to go. She smiled. He'd been confident about what her response would be. He knew her well for only having known her a few days.

They clambered up into the buggy.

Levi flicked the reins, starting the mare off at a trot. "I would like to be home by lunch. I'm supposed to go in to work this afternoon."

"For the buggy tours?"

"Jah." He glanced at her. "Would you like to *cumme*?"

Lilah blinked. "I don't know. Would you get into trouble?"

He snorted. "Not likely. My boss would be thrilled to have you join us. He has told me that I could bring a brother or a friend if I wanted to."

"I'll think about it." It might be amusing. And, she had to admit, spending time with Levi that didn't include doing something that might get them shot or killed had its own appeal.

As planned, Levi pulled the buggy off the road before they arrived at her property. He hopped out, then held out a hand to assist her.

"One moment." He reached behind his seat. His arm bounced a few times as he searched for something. "Ah! There it is."

Curious, she leaned closer. He was holding a pair of binoculars. Well-used ones, judging by the scratches and dings on them.

"These will help me see if there are any snipers hiding in the trees today."

Oh, she hoped he didn't see any. She placed one hand over her stomach, trying to quell the queasiness.

"We'll use the cover of the trees to go in behind the barn," Levi whispered. "If I tell you to drop, fall on your stomach on the ground. Don't ask questions. I don't want you to get hurt because you didn't move fast enough."

Lilah didn't trust herself to answer, so she just nodded. His blunt words sounded harsh, but she knew him well enough to understand he didn't mean them to be. It was just the way he was, and truthfully, she appreciated his honest approach and lack of pretense. It was fast becoming one of the traits she admired most about him. And Levi Burkholder had many outstanding characteristics.

For a moment, she regretted the risk he was placing himself in for her. If he got hurt, or worse, she didn't know how she'd live with the guilt.

He offered, she reminded herself.

Mentally, she prayed for their safety and for *Gott* to guide and protect them.

Levi beckoned for her to follow him. She did her best to mimic his actions, trying to keep her steps as quiet as his as they walked through the woody area. Whenever there was a sound, they would immediately freeze and Levi would visually search for the source of the noise. Then they would continue walking. It made for a very slow trek to the back of the barn, but Lilah couldn't see that they had any other choice. Every few minutes, Levi would motion for her to stay back, and he would step closer to the tree line to use his binoculars. At these times she held her breath until he returned to her.

She was so antsy to reach the destination that she was actually shocked when she found herself reluctant to leave the relative safety of the trees. More than reluctant. Levi had come back from using his binoculars again, and she found herself momentarily unable to move her feet.

Levi moved to stand directly in front of her. She was mortified at her weakness.

"I can do this," she whispered.

"*Jah*, I know you can."

She jerked slightly when his hand touched her face. Gently, he lifted her chin to bring her gaze to his. "You are a strong woman, Lilah. But even strong people have obstacles they can't cross alone."

His hand left her face and drifted down to take her right hand in his left. She gripped his hand tightly.

"Ouch," he said mildly. "Ready?"

Suddenly, she sniffed. "Do you smell smoke?"

He lifted his head and inhaled. His head whipped around in the direction of the smell. "It's close."

Still holding hands, they ran to the back of the barn. A breeze blew a thick cloud of black smoke past where they were standing into the trees they had recently left. Creeping along the back of the barn, they edged their way to the corner. The smoke was thicker now. The acrid smoke was burning her eyes and the insides of her nostrils.

Rage furled inside her. Lilah knew what they would find even before they looked around the corner.

The debris pile which had once been the shed that had served as Jacob's office was now a roaring mass of flames. The thick smoke from the blazing pile smelled horrid, curling and clawing at the sky like a hideous monster.

As the flames reached higher, the fire was spreading. The dry grass and the tree soon began to burn. Sparks and embers jumped from the main fire.

"Lilah, the barn is on fire!" Levi pointed to the front of the barn. It had indeed caught fire.

"We have to go—now!" Lilah just grabbed Levi's hand and pulled him back away from the wall. She didn't have time to explain, but she knew what was kept in that corner of the barn. Amish *hauser* didn't use electricity, but they did use propane and other fuels. Right inside the barn, Jacob had built a shelf, a wooden shelf, where he stored their extra propane, oil and kerosene for the lamps they lit their *haus* with.

Levi didn't question her urgency. Picking up the pace, he ran with her.

They were almost to the woods when the structure exploded, sending Levi and Lilah hurtling to the ground.

ELEVEN

Lilah hit the ground hard. The breath was knocked out of her, and she knew she would have several bruises.

Groaning, she got to her knees. They couldn't stop. Already she could hear the crackling of the fire around them. The smoke filling the air sent her mind back to the night when her brother had died. Except now, along with the smoke choking her, it was the memories.

Turning her head, she coughed. Then she cried out in fear.

Levi wasn't moving. His head was bleeding. It was bleeding profusely.

Nee, this could not be happening again.

Grunting, she pushed herself up and staggered to her feet. She had to get Levi out of here. Fast. This fire was going to blaze out of control, and she and Levi would be stuck and roasted alive.

She thought about moving back out to the open, but then she paused. That fire couldn't have been going very long. Which led her to believe that whoever had set the shed afire, surely they were still in the area.

Either she would be dragging Levi out to face a sniper, or they could continue on through the woods and face fire.

If only Levi was awake. *Nee*, she was smart enough to make a plan without him. Although it would be an immense help if Levi would get up and walk. Even if she had to support his weight, that would be *gut*. She didn't relish the idea of dragging him.

Gott, *I could really use help. Please, let him wake up.*

Bending down, she grasped him firmly under his arms and began dragging him away from the fire, deeper into the trees. She had only managed to drag him ten feet when her back muscles began to burn in protest.

They weren't going to make it.

Desperate and too exhausted to think, tears streamed down her cheeks.

Levi groaned. She stopped. When he groaned again, she gently set him back down on the ground and scurried around so she could see his face.

"Levi? Levi! Please open your eyes! You have to walk or we'll both die."

She didn't expect it to work, so was shocked when his eyes popped open. They widened farther when he saw the flames.

"Gotta get up." He rolled to his knees and retched.

She held her clasped hands to her lips, praying silently. "What can I do?"

"I probably have a concussion," he gasped out. "Nothing you can do. You'll have to help me walk."

She could do that.

Together, they managed to get him into a standing position, although she couldn't have said how they accomplished that seemingly impossible task. Once he was on his feet, she rushed over to his left side and burrowed under his arm. He wrapped it around her shoulders while she grabbed him around his back with her right arm. It was worse than entering a three-legged race when heights were vastly different. Except the issue now wasn't height as much as it was Levi trying not to give her too much of his weight. Which resulted in Lilah constantly trying not to be yanked to the side.

"Levi, lean on me a little more."

He resisted for a few minutes, but finally

sagged slightly against her. Most likely due to being too weary to do otherwise. Her back began to sweat, her dress beginning to stick to her skin like glue.

Was it her imagination, or was it becoming warmer?

Throwing a desperate glance over her shoulder, her fears were confirmed. The fire was greedily eating the first couple of trees.

"Trees…are burning," she gasped out to Levi, struggling to increase their pace.

"The trees are alive, grass is wet. It rained recently," he rasped. "Slow progress."

Still, she noticed that he put more effort into moving rapidly.

Five minutes later, she nearly cried when the siren at the local volunteer fire department rent the air. The department was being dispatched. Please *Gott*, let it be to the fire, and not an EMT call.

It was still early enough in the morning that she hoped most of the volunteer firefighters were at home. Sometimes if a call went out during the day, there would not be enough available personnel and the next department would be dispatched. She relayed this information between gasps to Levi.

"How do you know this?" His breathing was ragged by now.

"Jacob was in the department. The bishop allowed him a pager for such calls."

When she heard the unmistakable blare of the fire engines, she smiled. "The fire trucks are on their way."

They continued toward where the buggy had been left. Although they were still moving as fast as they could, some of the urgency had dissipated. The firefighters would take care of the threat at their backs. Even as they continued in their oddly staggering march, the heavy trucks rumbled past.

They were almost there.

The buggy, though, was not.

"Would your mare have taken off?" Lilah asked, a doubtful note creeping into her voice.

"She's never done that before." He looked around. "Although, I don't really have another explanation."

"So—" she ran her tongue across her teeth, giving herself a few seconds to think "—she ran away?"

He shook his head. "I don't know. Maybe. Or maybe she was scared by the explosion. Either way, we're stuck out here."

"It took me almost thirty minutes on foot to get to your barn."

By silent consent, they moved closer to the road. She set her jaw and hefted his arm tighter over her shoulders. They hadn't gone far when they heard someone crashing wildly through the woods behind them.

Levi shoved her down behind a thick tree, then knelt in front of her. Leaning in, he whispered in her ear. "I think we're being followed. There's no way we can outrun them."

She understood. Their only chance of not getting caught was to hide.

"Shouldn't you get down?"

He shook his head. "I'm going to see if I can see his face."

"Levi—" She broke off when the crashing drew closer. Whoever was following them was almost there.

Levi tensed, hearing their stalker coming. *Ack*, this guy would never have made it in the army. He ran after them with more noise than a stampede of elephants.

Briefly, Levi grinned, remembering Lilah comparing him to a rhinoceros. They were really into pachyderm analogies lately.

The smile bled from his face when the man

entered the woods. His jaw dropped. The man who was chasing them was no man at all, but a woman.

He blinked, thinking maybe she was just an innocent trying to escape the blaze. That idea died quickly as she paused and swung in a slow circle. He saw the gun strapped at her side. Her glare canvassed the area. He had no doubt she was searching for them.

He squatted lower, hoping to evade her glance. The adrenaline surged in his veins. His military training urged him to rush her.

A branch cracked off to the right. Levi moved nothing but his eyes, peeking out of the corners. A second hunter came into view. This one was holding a rifle in his very capable hands. All thoughts of ambushing those searching for them flew out of his mind. One person, he could handle. Even with a weapon, he would have surprise on his side.

Two? *Nee*, that would be foolish. He would probably be dispatched within seconds, leaving Lilah completely vulnerable. As much as he wanted to charge in, the wisest course of action would be to wait until these two were gone.

That didn't mean he couldn't take advantage of the fact that neither of them had seen him and try to memorize their appearance so he could report each detail to the police.

"Are you sure someone was out here?" the man growled. "I don't see anyone. I think you're imagining things, Tammy. We're wasting time."

"They left their buggy on the side of the road," the woman, Tammy, hissed. "I scared the horse away, so they have to be here somewhere. And keep your voice down. I didn't set that fire so you could warn them off with a tale to tell the cops."

They continued to argue softly for a few minutes. Levi filed their conversation away in his brain. They would indeed take this tale to the police.

Supposing they survived. He shoved the unworthy thought aside.

After what seemed like hours, the two began to wander away from where Levi and Lilah crouched. His legs and back were burning with the strain of keeping still, yet he didn't twitch so much as a muscle.

Finally, the noises from the two would-be assassins faded away.

"They certainly don't have your skill of walking quietly," Lilah remarked in a whisper.

He smiled. "That's an understatement."

He stood, holding in a groan as his muscles protested. He held his left hand down to her. She hesitated, then placed her slender hand in his and allowed him to assist her to her feet.

"Oh! My leg is asleep." When she wobbled slightly, he pulled her close to steady her.

Not a *gut* idea. Standing so close, he fought to remember why he couldn't lean in and kiss her.

Lilah pulled back and saved him from making that mistake. Her face was flushed. Averting her eyes, she laughed. A low breathless sound that captivated him.

"Which way should we walk?"

He mentally shook himself. "Let's walk back toward your property. It's opposite of the direction those two were heading."

She nodded. "How's your head?"

"It hurts some. I don't know if I can walk all the way to my *haus*." He took a careful step on his own. "I can walk without help now."

His legs were fine. And even though his head still ached, his vision wasn't blurry any longer. He was fairly sure he had a concussion.

The corners of her mouth tipped downward. She walked beside him for about a hundred feet before commenting. "I think your head hurts more than just 'some.' How are you going to work this afternoon?"

He'd forgotten about his job. "I don't know if I'll be able to make it in. When we have the opportunity, I'll use a phone to call my boss. He'll have to find someone else to drive tonight. Maybe I can switch with one of the other tour drivers."

Right now, that was the least of his concerns. The scent of smoke was still in the air.

"I think we should avoid coming out near where the fire was." Levi picked his way carefully through the brambles. Lilah's skirt caught on the prickly thorns a few times. She yanked it away fiercely. He grinned, surprised that he could find anything amusing. "That dress won't last very long if you don't take better care of it."

She screwed up her mouth and nose in the most adorable look of disgust he'd ever seen. "It will never come clean after this, anyway."

After that, their conversation died away.

Levi's ears caught the sounds of engines rumbling and conversation, interrupted by the beeps of radio static.

"I hear the first responders," Lilah commented, echoing his thoughts.

"*Jah*. We'll be ready to go home soon." His spirits lifted at the thought.

Five minutes later, they broke through the trees. Levi halted, stunned. Lilah gasped beside him.

The barn, or what was left of it, was in splinters. Some of the pieces had been flung as far as where the rubble from the *haus* lay.

"How did we survive that?" he said, his tone hushed with awe and shock.

"*Gott* saved us." Lilah trembled beside him. Whether from shock or exhaustion, or a mixture of both, he wasn't sure.

Levi reached out and took her hand. She clenched her fingers around his. He winced. She had a mighty strong grip when she was emotional. He didn't protest. If she needed to hold on to him, he'd let her. For as long as necessary.

TWELVE

They weren't able to get away as early as he'd hoped.

When they crashed through the trees, Levi and Lilah had stood, taking in the utter devastation of what had been her home for maybe a minute. Two minutes at the most. One of the firefighters had seen them and had shouted for them to stay where they were.

"Where exactly does he think we are going to go?" Lilah leaned into him as she spoke. Levi doubted she knew what she was doing.

"Let's just answer their questions. Hopefully, this won't last too long."

Watching the forceful gait of the firefighter striding toward them, he knew he was being overly optimistic. They were in for a long day.

The firefighter halted in front of them. Levi forced his impatience down while they endured his scrutiny. The man's gaze intensified as it took in the scratches and dirt covering them. When it landed on Levi's head, concern edged its way in.

His injury must be a mess. It sure felt like it was.

"You two know anything about this fire?" The man's voice was deceptively calm, as if he were asking about the weather or their favorite restaurant.

"Levi, I see Officer Dawson." Lilah slid the comment in before he could answer the firefighter.

Levi twisted his head to look where she was pointing. Officer Dawson was there, involved in a deep conversation with the fire chief.

"We need to speak with her," Levi informed their questioner. The man's mouth flattened. He might not like it, but Levi was tired and ached too much to care. "This is all part of another case she is working on. Trust me, she'll want to know."

Scowling, the man left them and sauntered over to the female cop. Her eyes widened and her head whipped around to see them. Nodding, she motioned for the chief to join her as she strode in their direction.

"Levi. Lilah. I didn't expect to see you so soon."

Was there disapproval in her voice?

"You had said the crime scene was cleared," Lilah ventured. Levi disliked the despair that crept into her voice. "I wanted to come and take another look at the shed. When we got here, it was on fire."

Levi took over when she stuttered to a stop, explaining about the fire and the explosion.

"What caused the explosion?" Her eyes were intent.

Lilah sighed. Without thinking, Levi hooked his left arm around her shoulders and hauled her close so she could rest against his side.

"That might have been an accident." She didn't sound so sure. "We kept our propane and our kerosene on a shelf right inside the barn."

Officer Dawson shook her head. "I disagree. I think that he—"

"She," Levi butted in. "Pretty sure the arsonist was a she."

"Okay. Let's start with the fire itself. The chief here tells me that the arsonist used an accelerant. Probably kerosene. A trail was left between the debris where the fire started and the barn. My guess is she used your kerosene, knowing that it was kept there, hoping to confuse the matter."

"You think she planned for the barn to explode." Levi rubbed Lilah's shoulder, silently offering comfort and support.

"I'm almost positive none of it was an accident. Now we have to decide why." She caught them both with a level stare. "It's your turn. Why are we looking for a female arsonist?"

Briefly, Levi and Lilah related the conversation they'd overheard while hiding from the two who were hunting for them.

"Tammy. Hmm. Tammy." Officer Dawson tapped her chin. "We have a name. And you say you got a good look at both of them?"

"*Jah*, I did," Levi confirmed.

"My back was to them," Lilah admitted. "I couldn't turn around to look without giving away our position."

Officer Dawson excused her with a wave of her hand. "One of you did. That should be enough. I will need you two to come with me to the station. If we have either of these two in our database, you could pick them out. It would make it much easier to solve this and find out who killed Jacob."

Levi and Lilah exchanged glances. When Lilah nodded, Levi said, "*Jah*. We will *cumme*."

"Wait!" Lilah said. "Before we go, my brother said there had been something in his office. I just remembered, after his office had been broken into a few years ago, he had been concerned that his confidential papers would be at risk. Jacob had had a special compartment dug into his floor. The shed might be gone, but it's possible that whatever he buried in that compartment is still there."

There was no mistaking the excitement dawning on Officer Dawson's face. "If you're right, whatever the arsonist was looking for— it might still be there. Wait here."

The police officer hurried away. They saw her grab her partner and watched as the two of them engaged in a high-energy conversation. Several times she pointed to where the shed had stood. Her partner pivoted and ran toward the still smoldering shed, yelling for the fire chief.

Officer Dawson ran back to where she'd left them. "Okay, it's being taken care of. I'm sorry to tell you, Lilah, this is once again a crime scene. So, you two will have to come with me as soon as the fire chief officially declares this arson, which he will. Believe me. But as soon as that happens, we're going to bring in some samples of the debris and dig up that compartment. If this all goes well, we should have whatever your brother buried by the end of the day."

Levi looked at Lilah. He knew she would hate having her home designated a crime scene again. However, they were close to getting answers. That had to be a relief.

Officer Dawson looked him over once more. "I'm also thinking we should stop by the hospital and have you two looked over. Levi, that injury on your head looks like it could be nasty." Part of him wanted to ignore her advice. They were wasting so much time. He squelched the urge to protest. Despite his impatience, he had to be prudent. If he was seriously injured and became incapacitated, what good would he be then?"

Reluctantly, Levi agreed with the police officer's suggestion.

There was one positive aspect to all of this, though. "Well, at least we have a ride now."

Lilah reached up and pinched his arm hanging over her shoulder.

"Oomph. What was that for?"

She shook her head as if disappointed, but the corners of her mouth were twitching.

Officer Dawson drove to the hospital first. Levi wasn't happy when he and Lilah were separated. He waited for nearly two hours to be seen. The doctor who came in brought a clinical student with him. Levi shifted uncomfortably as the doctor discussed him with the student as if he were a fascinating science experiment. When the examination was complete and his discharge papers were signed, he couldn't leave the room fast enough.

Officer Dawson was waiting inside the waiting room for him.

"Where's Lilah?" He scanned the room and the hallway. His mouth went dry.

"Relax. She was called back to see a doctor a few minutes ago. It might be a while. You were more of an emergency because of the head wound."

He forced himself to sit. Lilah was gone for over an hour. The moment she returned, he stood, ready to leave. Officer Dawson stood at a more leisurely pace.

Lilah reached up and gently touched the bandage on his head. Levi froze. "Is it bad?" she asked.

He didn't want to move. "*Nee.* I have a concussion. The doctor told me not to go to work for the next couple of days. If my head stops hurting, I can go back on Thursday."

She dropped her hands to her side. "I'm glad. I was worried."

"*Jah*, I knew you were. *Danke*, but I'm fine. Really."

"Now we can go to the station," Officer

Dawson announced. "I called ahead, so we can start working as soon as we arrive. The way I see it, the sooner we get done, the sooner you two can go home."

That sounded *gut* to him. Levi was ready for life to get back to normal.

Except that would mean no Lilah.

Suddenly, going back to his normal life was a bleak prospect.

Lilah didn't know what she expected the police station to look like. Maybe she expected that all the officers would have their own little office, a private place to work. When Officer Dawson led them into the main room at the station, she was surprised to see so little space between each desk.

Not that there were a lot of desks. They were just a little more crowded than she expected. Officer Dawson greeted an officer sitting at a desk piled high with files and general clutter. Seeing Lilah's amazement, she chuckled and pointed to another desk. This desk was the antithesis of the desk they had just passed. Everything was in its place, and the center of the desk was empty except for a closed laptop situated precisely in the center. There were no picture frames, nothing really personal. It was the epitome of an efficient work center.

"That's my desk. I can't function with any sort of clutter."

Lilah nodded. She approved of the cleanness and organization. What hurt her, though, was that the desk said nothing about the officer who worked at it. It could have been a desk for anyone to sit at.

Officer Dawson didn't stop at her desk. The carpeted floor masked the sound of her heels as she continued to a door near the back of the room. Entering, they saw a large conference table surrounded by several chairs. A laptop was set up on the table.

"Go ahead and take a seat. Next to each other, preferably."

Lilah and Levi each pulled out a chair and sat down side by side at the table. Officer Dawson fiddled with the laptop for about half a minute before setting it back down in front of them.

"This is a database where we keep images and profiles of known felons. I'd like you to go through and see if any of these individuals match the two you saw today. This is not something that you have to do quickly. Take as much time as you need. If you need a break, or if you need to walk around, we can do that before we get started. Can I get you something to drink?"

Levi and Lilah both requested water. Officer Dawson left to get their drinks.

"Are you okay with this?" Levi asked in a low voice.

"I guess. It's a little intimidating. Never been in a police station before."

"Me, neither. Let's get this done and go home."

That was easier said than done. It was terrifying how many people were on the database. They clicked on each page. They searched for a full forty-five minutes. Suddenly, Levi stopped.

"That's her," he said, staring intently at the image before them. "That's the woman I saw. Tammy."

Tammy was short for Tamera. Tamera Dawn Spitts.

"Are you positive that's the woman you saw?" Officer Dawson marked the name and information on the file.

"*Jah*, I'm sure. I had a clear view of her, and I watched her for several minutes."

"I can have her brought in for questioning. Why don't you keep looking? See if you can find the man she was with." Officer Dawson went out the door, closing it behind her with a soft click.

Lilah sat next to Levi, watching as he went through page after page. Could he feel the way the tension ramped up when the police officer left? His eyes remained focused on the images before him, but she knew he was aware of her at his side. Several times, he reached out and touched her shoulder or her hand. It was a gesture of comfort. But she had to wonder, was he offering consolation or seeking it?

She knew he'd been through some dark times. He had confronted evil in a way she could never imagine, even after what she'd been through. With every page, his face grew just a little more drawn.

He forwarded to the next page. Not content to just watch anymore, Lilah stretched out her hand and took hold of his left hand, squeezing it tight.

His fingers wrapped around hers. In some ways, it was as intimate and as healing as an embrace.

"I need to turn to the next page." There was a new huskiness to the texture of his voice.

He probably meant for her to release his hand. Instead, she continued to hold on tight while she brought her other hand up to move the screen forward. They continued that for the next few slides.

"That's him."

Lilah leaned forward in her chair.

The man in question was lanky with thick dark hair that fell over his forehead. He had a narrow face with hollowed out cheeks and deep squint lines near his eyes. His eyes—they looked like those of someone who'd be able to kill another.

She was shocked that she'd even had such a thought. Lilah wasn't one to think ill of those she didn't know. Although, technically, she knew of him, since she'd overheard his casual conversation with Tammy.

How were these people connected with Jacob? She'd never seen anyone suspicious hanging around the *haus*. So, if he was meeting them, or involved with them, it must have been during those times when he'd worked late.

The door creaked open and Officer Dawson slipped back into the room. She glanced over at the table.

"I found him," Levi announced without expression.

Lilah knew better. She could feel the stress strumming through him by the way his grip on her hand tightened. His handsome face was taut.

The fact that they were dealing with hard-ened criminals willing to kill seemed very real when she saw the face of those hunting them. She could no longer pretend, even in her own mind, that Jacob's death had been an accident.

Officer Dawson took down the name and information of the man. This time she didn't ask if he was sure he had the correct person. Going to the door, she called out to one of the other officers and handed the information off.

Returning to the table, she lowered herself into a chair across from Levi and Lilah.

"I thought you should know," she began, looking directly at Lilah, "I have gotten off the phone with the hospital. Ben and Waneta Hostetler are both making progress. Waneta should be able to return home this weekend. Ben will have to stay a few more days, but he will recover."

Lilah blinked as her lids burned with tears. *Thank You,* Gott. "Will she be all right by her-self?"

"Don't you worry about that. We've already talked with her children. One of them is com-ing down with his family to stay in the home for a few days."

"What about Hannah?" Worry for her sister-in-law gnawed at her.

The officer leaned forward with a smile. Her eyes stared straight into Lilah's. "We're not giving up on her. Even as we speak, officers are out looking for her."

Relieved, she rested back against the seat. She felt Levi's gaze on her face. Lifting her head, she saw his concern and smiled, letting him know she was fine.

Officer Dawson cleared her throat. Lilah blushed, breaking the contact with Levi. She hadn't realized she was staring.

Lilah frowned. "I hear a duck quacking."

She felt ridiculous making such a statement, but it was true.

The officer laughed and drew out her phone. When she answered, the ring was cut off mid-quack. "Hey, Lewis. What you got for me?"

Her grin faded. Intense satisfaction and excitement bloomed on her face.

She hung up and looked directly at Lilah and Levi. "You were right. Your brother had buried something under the floor of the shed. They're bringing it in now."

For a moment, Lilah forgot how to breathe. This could be it. She might finally learn why Jacob was killed.

She wasn't sure she wanted to know.

THIRTEEN

Lilah jumped to her feet, breathing fast. She braced her hands on the table to keep steady. She didn't feel she could handle this sitting down, yet was afraid she'd slip to the floor while standing up. She was alone and about to face a truth that might shatter her.

She was not ready for it.

A warm hand landed on her shoulder. She bowed her head and lowered her lids, gratitude filling her soul. Levi was here. He would stay with her. In this station full of strangers who didn't know her brother, he was here and would understand.

An officer entered the room, carrying a dust-covered black metallic box in hands covered with gloves. It had a handle, and on the front, there was a spot to enter a combination code.

She had never seen that box before in her life. Her shoulders tightened as the officer lowered the box onto the table. Lilah stared at it like it was a venomous snake poised to strike.

"Lilah?" Officer Dawson circled the table to stand on the other side of her. "Have you ever seen this box?"

She shook her head but couldn't seem to look away from the box. "*Nee.* I have never seen it before. I didn't know it existed until today."

Officer Dawson turned to the other police officer. "Lieutenant Quinn, can I ask how this was found, sir?"

Lilah finally removed her gaze from the box to see the other police officer. Until Officer Dawson had addressed him, she hadn't realized that he outranked the other police officer.

Lieutenant Quinn gave Lilah a reassuring smile. He must have seen how nervous she was. "Just like the young lady said, when we removed what was left of the shed, we found a compartment under the floor. It was almost like a very small cellar. We didn't have a key for it, so we broke into it and this box was the only thing there."

"Have you looked inside it yet?" Was that tiny voice really hers?

Levi rubbed her shoulder.

"No. If you know the combination, we won't

have to break the box. I thought we would try that first."

Lilah looked doubtfully at the box lying on the table. "I don't know the combination. Like I said, I didn't even know Jacob had this box."

Both police officers frowned and exchanged glances.

"Lilah, is there anything you can think of that your brother might have used? The combination is four numbers," Officer Dawson entreated.

Lilah hated to disappoint the officer. She had been so kind and patient. But she didn't have a clue. What four numbers would have been important to her brother? An idea popped into her head.

"Maybe let's try his wedding date." She rattled off the month and day when Jacob had married Hannah. Lieutenant Quinn punched the numbers into the keypad. When he attempted to open the box, nothing happened. The combination had not worked.

Lilah admitted to being disappointed. As much as she was afraid to see what was in the box, there was part of her that needed to know.

Officer Dawson looked at her. "Any other numbers you can think of?"

Lilah thought. She started to shake her head,

then stopped. An ice-cold chill went down her spine. A day that she would always remember, but wanted to forget, popped into her mind.

"Try April 27." The day her parents were killed.

The lieutenant tapped in the new code. A soft click came from inside the box. "I think we have a winner."

The lieutenant opened the box and extracted the contents.

From where she was standing, Lilah couldn't make out what he had. Mostly, it looked like a stack of receipts. There was a logbook, similar to the one Jacob had kept in his office, where he kept notes of all his transactions and communications with customers. Lieutenant Quinn opened the book and started reading the first few entries. His mouth dropped open and he motioned for Officer Dawson to read the entries.

When Officer Dawson had read them, she and Lieutenant Quinn exchanged glances. Lilah was concerned. Both their faces had gone very serious.

"What does it say?" Her voice was hoarse. "What was my brother into?"

Lieutenant Quinn cleared his throat. "This logbook is a diary of all sorts of communications between your brother and Billy Whitman. Specifically, starting a little less than five years ago, your brother started purchasing prescription pain medications from Billy."

Lilah stared. "We were in an accident. My parents were killed, and Jacob and I were both injured. We both had prescriptions for pain medication. It was a onetime prescription, no refills."

Officer Dawson sighed. "I'm sorry to tell you this, Lilah. Apparently, your brother became addicted to the painkillers. He could no longer get the drugs legally, so he started purchasing them from Billy. He was caught on tape making a drug deal. When he realized how far he had fallen, he agreed to become a source."

"I don't understand. What exactly does that mean?" Lilah asked.

Levi leaned forward. "He started helping the cops, didn't he?"

Both officers nodded. Officer Dawson replaced the book in the box. "He was working with one particular cop. It was one of those deals where none of the other cops knew who he was. Hopefully, this will help us find who's responsible."

Levi broke into the conversation. "But you have Billy in jail."

The lieutenant nodded. "True. But Billy is just a small player. See, we knew that Billy was dealing, but we also know that he is working for someone else. We're all trying to find the man who's running this operation."

"Are you telling me my brother wasn't doing anything bad?"

"No," Officer Dawson responded immediately, shaking her head. "In the logbook, he detailed his conversations with your bishop. He had the bishop's approval. The bishop and the cop involved had a conversation about the other criminal activity the leader of this group was dipping his hands into. Some of that activity could have affected the Amish community. The bishop had agreed as long as helping the police did not compromise Jacob or lead him into doing drugs again. He had kept his end of the bargain."

Lilah frowned. Her head was starting to ache again.

"Then why kill him?"

"That's the last entry. He wrote that he felt he could no longer continue with a baby on the way. So, he was going to give all his evidence to the police and break all connection with the drug dealers. My guess, he was either seen talking to the cop or he confronted Billy personally."

Lilah clenched her fists together to keep from breaking apart. She was happy that Jacob hadn't been in the wrong, that he was trying to help others. That was completely what she'd expect from him. On the other hand, how had she not known about his previous addiction?

She remembered how it felt when she had taken the painkillers herself. She had been sleepy and had lost the ability to focus. Why hadn't she noticed a change in Jacob?

It struck her as horribly sad to have all these questions and know that she would never have the answers.

If Levi had to say what the expression on Lilah's face was, *devastated* would be the only word he'd be able to think of. He wasn't sure which part of this new information was the most painful to her. Certainly, the idea that Jacob had suffered with an addiction before breaking free of it was painful. He'd seen first-hand how addiction could destroy people's lives.

Or maybe it was the fact that Jacob had been working, sort of undercover, with the police

and she never knew. Maybe that was the part
that bothered her the most.

It was also possible that she was devastated because she had finally realized that her
brother was never coming home again. Sometimes it took a while for that truth to sink in.
When it did, there was always an emotional
crisis of some kind.

"Are you going to be all right?" he whispered to her.

"I don't know. I feel a little lost right now."
He knew she was struggling when she admitted it to him. Reaching over, he wrapped both
arms around her. He thought she might with-
draw from him, but she didn't. Rather, she settled against him with a sigh. He dropped his
chin on the top of her *kapp* and just held on to
her, letting her feel his strength.

Both officers quietly excused themselves,
giving Levi and Lilah some privacy. He appreciated their sensitivity. After a couple of minutes, she stirred in his arms. He loosened his
grip but didn't completely let go. Lilah leaned
back and looked him in the eyes.

"*Danke*, Levi."

He brushed a tendril of her blond hair back
away from her forehead. Her face grew warm
beneath his fingers. It would be so easy to lean

in and kiss her, the way he longed to do. He fought the temptation, knowing that kissing her when he didn't feel able to court her would be wrong. Lilah was a woman who deserved to be respected and cherished.

He wished he could be that man. He was finding it impossible to keep his emotions under control.

She had wormed her way into his heart with her sweet ways and her courage. He didn't know if he'd be whole when they went their own ways, but he would do his best to keep his distance, for her sake.

Reluctantly, he dropped his arms and returned to his seat when the door opened. Lilah remained where she was. Had she decided to keep her distance from him? He was aware of the irony that no sooner had he decided to keep his distance than he became irritated that she might have decided to take the same action.

"When can we go home?" He couldn't remember the last time he'd been this drained. Physically, emotionally. Everything about this day had sucked the energy clean out of him. He wanted to go to his *haus*, hug his *mamm*, eat some of her cooking and go to bed to sleep for a week.

He also wanted to find a way to avoid being

too close to Lilah, and that wasn't likely to happen until this mess was over. Because no matter how hard it was being around her, it would be worse knowing danger was near her and being unable to assure himself of her well-being.

"We can give you a ride home in about five minutes." Lieutenant Quinn opened the door and went halfway through before halting again. "Oh, by the way…the man you identified, Pete Oliver, he's been wanted for a long time on drug and murder charges. We didn't know he was back in the area. It's likely that he's the one running the operation."

"Which means if you catch him—" Lilah started.

"If we catch him, the operation goes belly-up and you're safe to return to your life without fearing someone is after you."

Levi wanted that for her. He wanted Lilah to feel safe. To be able to dream and to laugh frequently.

Just not with him.

Lieutenant Quinn was as good as his word. Five minutes later, he entered the conference room again, this time wearing jeans and a black T-shirt. He had traded his smart hard-soled police issue shoes for a well-worn pair of sneakers. He sauntered over to the coffee-pot and refilled his coffee.

"I'm ready whenever you two are."

"I'm ready." Lilah stood gracefully and strode to the door.

"*Jah*, me, too."

They walked out to the back parking lot together. Between the hospital and the time spent looking over the database, they had missed most of the day.

"Supper will be on the table before we get to my *haus*," Levi remarked.

"Your *mamm*, will she be worried?" Lilah's brow creased.

"Nah. I told her I didn't know how late we'd be today. Of course, I had no plans on getting hit by an exploding barn, but she knows we might not make it until late."

Lilah snorted. "A piece hit you. You make it sound like the whole barn landed on you."

He winked at her. It was *gut* hearing her laugh.

Levi grinned and smacked his hands together when he saw Lieutenant Quinn's truck. A full-size Ford F-150 pickup truck. "Man! You have *wheels*!"

Lilah rolled her eyes. "I'm sure it has four-wheel drive."

The officer laughed. "Yes, ma'am. You can't go through winter in this part of the country without it."

Levi hadn't been kidding when he told Lilah the one thing about the *Englisch* world he missed was four-wheel drive. "Lilah, I used to drive one of these when I was *Englisch*. It was sweet."

Lieutenant Quinn raised an eyebrow and smiled. Levi could see that he didn't know if Levi was being serious.

"Well, then you're in for a treat. Hop in. I need to make one stop along the way."

They piled in the truck and headed out. Levi itched to get in the driver's seat. They stopped at a small convenience store in town so Lieutenant Quinn could pick up a gallon of milk before he went home.

Levi and Lilah waited in the truck for him. The silence was rife with tension. That kiss that never happened was lingering between them.

"I need to stretch my legs," Levi said, just to get out of the truck.

He stood outside, looking up at the stars. When he heard a jingle, he dropped his gaze to see Lieutenant Quinn heading his way. He made to go back to the truck.

The first bullet knocked the milk out of Lieutenant Quinn's hand. The second, as the lieutenant threw himself in front of Levi, hit the lawman in the chest.

FOURTEEN

Levi caught Lieutenant Quinn as he fell. Shouting for Lilah to open the door, he dragged the injured cop to the truck. With Lilah's help, they managed to get him inside.

The store attendant had rushed out, a rifle in his hands. If he hadn't been there, Levi doubted they would have survived.

"I called for help."

A car screeched down the road toward them.

"No time!" Levi jumped into the cab behind the wheel. "Go inside and lock the door. This is a cop. I'm driving to the hospital," Levi said to the store owner.

"Keys, keys, where are the keys!"

"In the ignition!" Lilah twisted in her seat. "Levi!"

The back window shattered. Twisting the keys to start the engine, Levi floored it. The truck shot forward. He spun out of the parking lot and into the street. A horn blared as he cut off a car coming from the opposite direction.

"Sorry, sorry." Sweat trickled down his face. "Is he breathing?"

Lilah leaned closer to Lieutenant Quinn. "He's breathing, but his color is *schrecklich*."

That was not *gut*.

He sent up a silent prayer for help. A roar from the rear alerted him that the shooter was behind him. The light ahead was green. He pushed his foot down on the gas, desperate to put some space between him and the man, or woman, coming after them. It had to be Pete Oliver or Tammy Spitts. No one else had any reason to want them dead. He couldn't seem to pull away from them. They were two car lengths away from the light when it switched to yellow.

"Hang on!" Levi hollered. Pushing the gas pedal clear down to the floor, he shot toward the light. It changed red as he was clearing the intersection. Lilah grabbed Lieutenant Quinn and held him tight. She gasped as a car coming from the other direction missed them by less than a foot.

He didn't know that he loved four-wheel drive anymore. This kind of excitement was the kind he would happily live without.

A quick look cast over to Lilah showed that her face was pale, but her jaw was set. That was his Lilah. Strong and capable. She would not falter in the midst of danger. He knew he could rely on her to watch over Lieutenant Quinn while he took care of the driving.

The traffic going the opposite way leaned on their horns. He glanced in the rearview mirror. They hadn't lost their tail. The shooter had run the red light right behind Levi. Levi spun the wheel, taking a hard left. He hoped the oncoming traffic would slow the other vehicle down.

It did, but not enough to matter.

The car kept pace with him no matter where he went.

"We have to get him to a hospital," he yelled over the engine. "I'm hoping the shooter behind us won't follow us into the emergency room. I'd wait, but I think Quinn will die if he doesn't get there soon."

The car continued to trail after them as they turned and swerved, one street after another. It could have been worse. Instead of gaining on them, the vehicle was keeping up, sometimes getting closer, but never overtaking them.

Sirens burst out behind them. Flashing lights pulsed, flaring red, white and blue against the dashboard.

The convenience store attendant had come through for them. Finally, the car chasing them veered off. Two police cars lit off in pursuit.

A third car slipped around them, lights still on and sirens flashing.

"They're giving us an escort to the hospital to make sure we get there in time to save Lieutenant Quinn."

At the hospital, Levi drove under the emergency room awning. A paramedic was waiting at the door. At his shout, others came running. Obviously, someone had called in to expect them. Within seconds, they were swarmed with medical personnel. Lilah jumped down so they could get Lieutenant Quinn out of the vehicle.

It was amazing how gently and efficiently they extricated Lieutenant Quinn from the truck and placed him on the stretcher. Within seconds, he was whisked back inside the hospital, the automatic doors whooshing closed behind them.

Lilah started to climb back up into the cab. Levi halted her.

"I need to go and park this truck. Please go into the hospital and wait for me. There might be information the police or the doctors need to give us."

She gave him a doubtful look but didn't

complain. Backing away from the vehicle, she shut the door and ran to the electronic doors, pausing only long enough to allow them to open for her before dashing inside to the safety of the hospital.

He didn't blame her. After what had just happened, he felt exposed out here himself. That was the real reason he sent her inside. The parking lot was crowded. The last thing he wanted was to have her walking that distance, vulnerable to a sniper. He didn't know if the man had been caught yet or not.

Once Lilah was safely inside the building, Levi shifted the truck back into Drive, put his foot on the gas pedal, and gunned the engine more than he planned. Grimacing, he darted a glance around to see if anyone had noticed. No one was there. *Gut*. He had not had the opportunity to drive like this for a while. His skills were a bit rusty.

But still *gut* enough to have driven an injured police officer to the hospital, he reminded himself.

To his surprise, he found the thrill of driving a big truck was no longer as fun as it had once been. He was glad he'd possessed the ability at the critical moment when they were being shot at. But other than that, he didn't think he would miss it the way he had. Not now that he'd had the chance to drive again.

He'd be much happier driving his buggy with his mare.

It took him a while to find a parking space big enough for the large pickup truck. He shook his head every time he passed a spot that might have worked but had been rendered useless because someone had parked over the line.

Carelessness? He could see someone being distraught and not paying attention. Although he had known people who would deliberately take up two spaces so their car wouldn't get scratched by another driver.

You didn't have to worry about that with a buggy. It was plain and serviceable, so if it got a bit scratched or dinged, no one cared. As long as it worked.

Finally finding a spot, he turned off the engine. Sitting in the cab, he breathed deep for a moment. Saying a prayer for protection, he opened the door, hopped down and made a mad dash for the entrance. Dodging the parked cars, he weaved through the lot, not feeling safe until the doors whooshed shut behind him.

Lilah paced the waiting room. The doctors had rushed Lieutenant Quinn to surgery. A couple of police officers prowled the hallways. So far, no one had said much to her other than asking if she was well or if she needed something.

What she needed was Levi. Well, she needed to know he was safe, she clarified. Her mind mocked her. She ducked away from the knowledge of how much he was coming to mean to her, but she couldn't escape it.

Levi Burkholder had become very important to her in the few days they'd known each other. *Ach!* How could this have happened? She knew he was helping her because she was Jacob's little sister. He was being generous with his time, risking his life, but she wasn't foolish enough to believe there could be more. Every time they seemed to be getting closer, she felt a wall springing up between them.

This afternoon, at the police station, she had known he wanted to kiss her. Her heart had pounded. She hadn't backed away, hadn't wanted to. At the last instant, he'd drawn back and closed her out.

That had hurt—she couldn't deny it. When Lieutenant Quinn had walked in, she had been relieved. His presence had stopped her from doing or saying something she might have regretted.

Lilah's head dropped forward, the regret coming anyway. Except it was regret for having seen a fine police officer shot while protecting her. Protecting Levi.

Lilah had watched, horrified, those last few seconds when bullets rained down upon two very fine men.

"Lilah!" Levi rushed into the waiting room, his gaze starting around nervously.

"I'm all right." She looked past his shoulder, having trouble meeting his eyes. She couldn't let herself continue to be drawn to this man. He didn't want her in his life, not really.

"What's going on?"

Was it her imagination or did he sound confused?

"Lieutenant Quinn is in surgery. I haven't heard anything else."

She wasn't that surprised. After all, it had only been five minutes since he had dropped her off at the emergency door entrance. But those five minutes had seemed more like an hour.

Edgy and restless, she turned away and veered toward the window. She disliked hospitals immensely. Hadn't she spent more than enough time in one?

"I'm glad you weren't hurt." She felt more than saw Levi's presence at her side.

"*Danke.* I'm glad you weren't, either." She looked out the window. She longed to say more but held back. Finally, the pressure building inside her burst with a hiss. "I hate hospitals! The last time I was in one was the night Jacob died. Before that, I was in a hospital after the accident that killed my parents."

He sidled closer, offering her his silent support. A different kind of edginess slid along her nerves. She wanted what she could never have.

She should move, put more space between them. She couldn't. These random moments of closeness might be all she ever had with Levi. She'd have to cherish each and every one.

At the same time, she had to be careful. Talking was the best way to distract herself right now.

"After the accident, I had months of physical therapy. I came to the hospital for a few sessions, but that was very difficult. After that, the hospital allowed a physical therapist to *cumme* to the *haus*. It was during that time that Jacob must've become addicted to the painkillers. I had them, too, but I only took them for a couple of days because I didn't like the way they made me feel."

A wave of sadness nearly drowned her.

"How could I not have known? How could I not have seen how Jacob was suffering?"

Levi wrapped his arms around her and drew her close. She knew she should fight it, but she snuggled closer, sighing as his embrace wrapped around her like a warm blanket. If only for a moment, she felt loved and protected.

Was it her imagination, or did she feel a kiss on the top of her head? It was hard to tell while wearing her prayer *kapp*.

"You can't blame yourself, Lilah," Levi's low voice whispered. She shivered as his breath tickled her ear. His hold tightened in response. He must've thought she was cold. "Hannah didn't notice it, either. Otherwise, I doubt she would have married him."

She frowned. "Unless he'd already broken free of the addiction when they married. Officer Dawson didn't really say when he started working for the police."

She still had trouble believing that one. Although, it would have been in character for Jacob to try to help those who had suffered like he had. So maybe it was more credible than she had thought.

"My brain hurts from all this."

Levi's chuckle caught her by surprise.

"What's so funny?" As far she could tell, there was nothing humorous about their situation.

"It just sounded funny." His chin rested against her head. "I think I'm just really tired."

"*Jah.* I'm exhausted."

Finally, she backed out of his embrace. Foolishly, the moment his arms dropped away from her, she wanted them back again.

Looking down, the light of the room flashed against the silvery cast of his right hand.

"You're amazing. You know?" She flushed. She hadn't meant to blurt that out. She blamed tiredness for affecting her, also.

Peeking up at him, she caught the astonishment stamped on his face.

"Me? There's nothing so amazing about me. I'm a simple man, doing the best I can. The same can be said of my father and my brothers."

"Well, I think the way you've gone out of your way to help me is amazing."

She let it go at that. How could she explain? She knew it had to be hard for him, suffering from PTSD, to be helping her when people were after them with guns.

She thought of something. The explosion hadn't triggered a flashback. She asked him about it.

"I don't know why. Maybe because I was out of it for a few minutes afterward. I'm glad I didn't. Not only for me, but if I had, we wouldn't have escaped."

Shuddering, she wrapped her arms around her middle. "*Gott* protected us, that is true."

He nodded but didn't say anything. The conversation died between them as they stood side by side, staring out at the parking lot.

Lilah started when she heard her name.

Officer Dawson had arrived. "Hey, are you okay?"

When they assured her that they were fine, she visually checked them over. Finally, apparently satisfied, she nodded. "Listen, you two really saved Quinn's life, acting so quick like you did. I just talked to a nurse. He's still in surgery, but they expect him to pull through." She tilted her head at Levi, her brow furrowing. "Say, you won't get in trouble for driving, will you? With your bishop, I mean."

Lilah blinked. She hadn't even thought of that.

Levi shook his head. "I don't think so. I have

permission from him to drive in my interactions with the *Englisch*. Besides, he would be all right with me saving a life." Levi scowled suddenly. "He was in danger because he was driving us to my parents' *haus*."

Remorse covered his face when Lilah flinched. "Hey. This is not your fault," Levi said.

Officer Dawson gave a sharp nod. "He's right, Lilah. You can't be responsible for the bad choices other people make. And Quinn? Even if you knew there had been a shooter out there, he still would've offered his help. It's what he does. I've never known him to back down, to save himself when someone else needed help."

Interesting. There was more than a little admiration in her tone. In fact, Lilah was fairly certain that the efficient Officer Dawson had some less than efficient feelings for the handsome lieutenant in surgery.

"Anyway, if you guys are ready to go, I can give you a ride back to your house."

"Before you go, what happened to the person chasing us?" Levi inquired softly.

Lilah blinked. For a second or two, she'd actually forgotten why they were there.

"Yes. It was Tammy Spitts. She demanded

a lawyer before we even got her in the police car. It's unlikely she'll give up Oliver so quickly. We strongly suspect he was the one shooting at you."

"I hadn't thought about it. But there had to have been two people," Levi mused. "The shots came from somewhere in front of us, but the car that chased us came up from the other direction. Maybe that's why we had time to get Quinn into the truck."

"What do you mean?" Lilah asked.

Levi quirked a smile at her. "The shooting stopped for a few seconds. The guy shooting at us probably had to call her, let Tammy know our exact location. Which means he couldn't get to us immediately."

"We still don't know how this was all set up."

Lilah fought back a yawn, but it still managed to work its way out.

"Okay, time to get you two home. The chief has agreed to let us patrol your street for the next couple of days, Levi. Nothing extreme. Just a car to drive by every hour or so."

Lilah didn't want to admit it, but knowing the police were looking out for them made her feel better. It would haunt her forever if something happened to Levi or any member of his family. She would never be able to accept that she wasn't to blame for that.

Five minutes later, they were heading back to Levi's *haus*. The weariness she'd pushed aside finally overcame her. Leaning her head back against the seat, she drifted off to sleep.

A gentle hand nudged her awake. Blinking, she opened her eyes, still drowsy, and smiled up at Levi.

"I fell asleep," she murmured.

"*Jah*. You were snoring."

That jolted all drowsiness out of her system.

Bolting upright, she glared at him in outrage. "I do not snore!"

Officer Dawson laughed. Lilah flushed. She'd forgotten that they weren't alone.

"Don't worry, you weren't snoring, Lilah." The pretty police officer gave her a small smile. "Much."

Grinning, Levi opened her door wider so Lilah could step out of the police cruiser.

They both thanked Officer Dawson for the ride and watched as she returned to the car.

"If I hear anything about Oliver, I'll be in touch," she promised.

Simultaneously, Levi and Lilah turned to go inside the *haus*. Fannie Burkholder was standing on the porch watching them. Concern lined her face.

"*Mamm?* Is something wrong?" Levi rushed to her side.

"Not anymore." She patted his cheek. "The mare returned hours ago without the buggy. All lathered like she'd been galloping. We were concerned you'd been in some sort of accident. Your *daed* and brothers are out looking for you."

Ashamed, Lilah realized she'd forgotten that Tammy had scared the horse away. It had never occurred to her to wonder if the animal would return home or not. Levi lifted stricken eyes to her. He hadn't thought of it, either.

"I'm sorry!" Agony twisted her voice, making it tight.

"*Nee*, all is well. You are home now."

The sound of a buggy on the road broke the silence of the early summer evening. David Burkholder drove the buggy into the driveway.

"Ah, *gut!*" Sam popped out of the buggy. "I told *Mamm* and *Daed* you were fine."

Abram followed with a smile, but his tight eyes searched Levi.

"I'm fine," Levi assured him quietly.

"*Jah!* All is well. David, *cumme esse!*" Fannie called him in to eat. "All our *kinder* are safe."

The older woman patted Lilah's shoulder. Heat collected in Lilah's cheeks as she realized she was included in that statement.

Without meaning to, Fannie had let her know, let them all know, that she saw Lilah as more than just Levi's friend. Lilah didn't know how to tell Fannie without sounding rude that she and Levi would never be more than friends. Because Levi wouldn't allow that to happen.

Dinner was awkward. At least, it was for Lilah. Every minute she sat at the table, the longing to truly become part of this family grew.

She excused herself and escaped to her bedroom as soon as possible. How had it happened? How had she fallen for Levi in just a few days? Weren't things like that supposed to take years?

But not only had she fallen for him, she now understood that if he were to ever think of her that way also, she would be accepted by the whole family. They had made that more than clear at dinner. Although, she wasn't sure Levi had caught all the winks and sly looks.

The family had been concerned, true. When

they explained what had happened, both Fannie and David had gone pale. The idea that someone was out there shooting at their son! But neither one of them had by a single look, expressed any inkling that they thought Lilah might be to blame for this. They were only glad to have both Levi and Lilah safe.

It also amazed her that neither one of them complained at the thought of having a police car doing drive-bys. It would probably have been a different story had an officer been planted at the *haus*, but just driving by seemed to be okay.

With a loud sigh, Lilah flopped over to her other side in the bed. As soon as she was safe, she had to leave. She didn't know where she would go yet.

All she knew was the longer she stayed, the deeper the heartache would be when she finally got away.

FIFTEEN

Levi was busy in the barn Thursday morning when he felt his father's presence. Although he was careful not to let his father see the expression, he grimaced. He'd been expecting *daed* to come have a talk with him since dinner Tuesday evening, after he and Lilah had survived the explosion and been shot at all in one day.

"*Sohn.*" David greeted him.

Levi ducked his head in response. He knew he should say something, but he couldn't think of anything that would be appropriate in the circumstances.

Finally, his *daed* broke the silence. "Your mother and I, we both have thanked *Gott* many times. We thanked him when he returned you to us. You had suffered horrible things, but you were home. We thanked him when you found your niche, and we thanked him again when you and Lilah arrived home safely the other night."

"*Jah*. I thanked *Gott*, too. He protected us."

"*Jah*, he did." His father paused, his gaze searching the wall of the barn as if he'd find the right words to say there. "Levi. You are no longer a boy."

Oh, no. Here it comes.

"It is time for you to settle down, to build a home of your own."

"*Daed*—"

"Your mother and I have watched you with the *maidal* in our community. You have been polite and kind. But other than that, it was clear you had no interest. Now we understand why. Levi, what do you plan to do about Lilah?"

"*Nee, Daed*. You don't understand. Lilah's brother was my friend. I am helping her until she finds out what happened. As soon as we know, she's leaving. I'll probably never see her again." He forced himself to say it, to face that she would leave him. Wincing as he said the harsh words, Levi couldn't stop himself from rubbing his chest with his left hand. The idea of her leaving struck him as a physical pain. His parents had obviously seen that he had formed an emotional bond with her. He hadn't planned to. He had struggled against it but had failed.

His one fear now was that it was one-sided, and that she didn't share the same feelings for him.

His *daed* watched him, disappointment gleaming in his dark eyes. "Levi, would you really throw away this gift *Gott* has given you?"

Startled, he jerked his face up to look at his *daed*. "Gift? What gift?"

Love and caring were great, but they also brought a huge risk. He remembered the months of anguish and doubt that followed Harrison's death. The feeling of letting his friend down, of being responsible for the tragedy, had followed him all the way back to the States.

How much worse would such agony be if something happened to his wife? Or his children?

It hit him then. He was already thinking about Lilah in terms of marriage. There was no way he was getting out of this situation with his heart intact.

"*Jah*, a gift," his father continued, unaware of the dark paths Levi's mind had just traveled. "A *frau, kinder*. Family. It is all a gift."

Levi shook his head. "I don't know that I want that kind of gift. There's no guarantee that I would be able to keep a wife safe, that she or one of my children would never get sick. Or worse."

"Maybe so."

Frustrated, Levi ran his hands through his hair. "Then what's the point? Why put yourself at risk when you can live free, without that kind of pain?"

David narrowed his eyes at his son. "Are you free? Listen to yourself. Do you sound like someone who is free and happy?"

Levi stilled. He didn't want to answer that question.

His father continued. "*Jah*, I know there is pain, ain't so? I have experienced it."

His sister, Marie. They rarely talked about her, but Levi remembered the older sister who had grown ill and died suddenly fifteen years ago. How could he be so cruel as to remind his father of his loss?

"I see what you are thinking, and you are wrong, my *sohn*." David's hand landed on his right shoulder. "We still miss our Marie, but we never forgot her. And we are thankful we had her, even for a short time."

Levi shrugged. He wasn't his father. Losing a friend had been agonizing, devastating. He didn't think he had it in him to risk losing a child or a spouse.

It was better to be closed off.

His father left him to continue working. As Levi tinkered with the car he was fixing, his mind kept flashing back to the conversation.

Lilah was in the house working with his *mamm*. It was a beautiful day, but Levi knew he wouldn't go in and ask her to go for a walk. The best course of action was to keep his distance.

The trouble was his heart didn't seem to agree with his head.

It was late evening when a police cruiser entered the driveway. Officer Dawson emerged. He went out to meet her, conscious that his entire family and Lilah were sitting together on the porch, listening to the conversation. The police officer waved at Lilah. The young Amish woman broke away from the rest of the group and came to join Levi on the driveway.

"Hi." Officer Dawson greeted them, a wide smile spreading across her face. "I wanted to tell you in person that we have Pete Oliver in custody."

The weight he'd been carrying fell off his shoulders.

"Lilah is safe now," Levi commented.

The officer's lips flattened. "I can't promise that. While we know that Oliver was involved, we don't have absolute proof that he was the leader yet. We're working to get it."

"It's *gut* news, though," Lilah remarked. "How is Lieutenant Quinn?"

The officer's cheeks flushed. "He's going to be fine."

As she left, Levi was struck with the realization that this was it. Lilah would be leaving. It was what he wanted, but it wasn't.

Then he remembered he'd made her one promise. He couldn't promise her a life together, but he could give her an afternoon.

"Do you still want to go with me on the buggy tour tomorrow?"

Her eyebrows climbed her forehead. She thought he'd forgotten. He pushed down the guilt. She had probably noticed his avoidance. It had to be that way.

But suddenly, the desire to have one more day in her presence, to bask in the sunshine of her personality one more time, was overwhelming.

"Are you sure you want to take me with you?" she asked.

He winced. *Jah*, she'd noticed.

"I want you to *cumme*. Really."

* * *

The next day, he had cause to second-guess his decision as she sat next to him. He couldn't help but imagine a lifetime of riding beside her. She'd washed her dress out yesterday. Her face was scrubbed clean and she had a small smile on her face as they drove into town.

She looked beautiful and serene. Content.

The urge to reach out and hold her hand swept through him. He fought it back. They were not courting. This was a goodbye activity.

He didn't like to think of that, but it was. For his peace of mind, it had to be.

As he'd expected, his boss was more than happy to allow Lilah to ride along with him. It made the tour seem more authentic. Levi curled his lip. It felt more real than he was comfortable with.

Their first customers that day were a group of authors on a research trip. He had to admit, it was fun showing them around. They were full of smart questions, and he could tell that they truly wanted to respect Amish culture by getting their facts correct. Lilah helped answer some of their questions. It was fun having her with him.

The second tour was harder to handle. A pair of newlyweds were his sole guests. They were more interested in staring at each other than anything he did to say. Lilah's cheeks burned bright red when their guests started a rather inappropriate conversation.

She glanced over her shoulder, then addressed him in Pennsylvania Dutch. "Don't they know they're not in private?"

He answered in the same dialect. "They don't care."

It bothered him, too. That kind of conversation should be private. In his way of thinking, it was a matter of respect for your spouse.

Except he wasn't ever getting married.

Finally, the tour ended. The couple left the buggy, said a distracted thank-you and departed. He looked up at Lilah. "We have one more tour, in about an hour. Let's go walk a bit, stretch our legs."

She climbed down and joined him. They walked along the sidewalk, looking at the various shops. They didn't talk about anything personal, and by mutual agreement, also avoided conversation regarding the danger of the past few days.

Levi didn't know if Lilah felt it, but he wasn't convinced about the danger being past. Maybe if Officer Dawson had been more convinced, he might have been at peace.

As they reached the corner, a car careened around the bend. Levi hauled Lilah up against him and pulled her against the building. The car continued on, rock music blaring from the open windows.

Teenagers. He growled in frustration. Looked down to inquire if she was all right, but the question never got asked.

Blue eyes were regarding him as if he were the most amazing thing she'd ever seen. A man could drown in a look like that.

Drawn beyond his power to resist, he lowered his head. When his lips met hers, he was lost.

Lilah's lids fluttered shut as Levi kissed her. She'd been courted, but had never been kissed in her life.

It was pure bliss, feeling the gentle caress of his lips against hers. The kiss was chaste, nothing more than a brush of skin, but she felt her heart speed up.

And then it was done.

Her eyes opened slowly. Levi's face was pale. The kiss had shocked him. The joy of the past few seconds dissipated, and despair swept in. He regretted the kiss. All the thoughts she'd entertained in the past day were true. He had been avoiding her. He felt their connection, but he didn't want it.

Tears gathered behind her lids, but she refused to let them fall. Lilah knew she had fallen in love with Levi, but she wouldn't beg for him to love her back. He had to want her in his life. He had been broken. She couldn't be the one to fix him. Only *Gott* could do that.

Pasting a smile she didn't feel on her face, she said, "We should go back, *jah*?"

Her heart broke further in her chest as he latched on to her suggestion. "*Jah.* We should go and wait for the next tour."

The next tour. How would she stand sitting so close to him on the bench of a buggy, chatting about Amish culture and customs, while her heart was shattering inside her?

She couldn't do it. The peace and closeness had turned to dust in her mouth.

Silently, she walked beside him, trying to figure out how she could get out of it. She couldn't ask him to take her home. Levi had a job to do. If he left, he could get fired. She wouldn't do that to him.

As they returned to the buggy, she stood aside as he checked it over and got the horse ready.

Suddenly, she felt light-headed, as the reality of what she was about to lose washed over her. This man had saved her, and she had fallen in love with him. Now she had to leave him. She had to walk away and leave him, and the pain ripped at her.

"Lilah?" Levi touched her cheek. She focused on him, trying to ignore the agony his gentle touch brought. *"Bist du krank?"*

Was she sick? At heart, she was.

"Nee. I'm a little light-headed."

Concern darkened his eyes. "Maybe I should bring you home."

"I don't want you to get in trouble." She looked around. "Look, I'll go and wait in that café there."

He followed where she was pointing. He started to protest, but she cut him off.

"Don't worry. I'll be inside, and you can find me when you *cumme* back. I think it will help me to get out of the sun and drink something. Maybe I'm dehydrated. When you return, I'll be fine."

He didn't look convinced. It took some doing, but she managed to convince him. She watched him as he greeted his next customers and climbed up on the bench.

He looked lonely.

She shook the thought away. She couldn't

help him. If Levi ever opened up enough to let someone in his heart, she'd gladly be part of his life.

But until that day...

He flicked the reins, and the mare pulled the buggy away. His gaze sought her out one more time. She smiled for his benefit. His brown eyes bore into hers for a moment before he looked away. The smile slid from her face the moment he was out of sight.

Sighing, she turned to go into the restaurant.

A hand grabbed her arm. Something jabbed into her back. Chills broke out. Her intuition told her it was a gun.

"Don't look at me, don't scream. Just start walking. Or I'll call someone to come and take care of your friend."

She understood. Levi would die if she didn't go. If she did, then he had a chance to survive. She started walking. Sweat poured down her back and beaded on her forehead. The knot in her stomach continued to grow, twisting and turning. Her legs shook, not from exhaustion, but from terror.

She was going to die. She sent a prayer winging to *Gott*. Give her strength. Protect Levi and his family.

She hadn't told him she loved him. Now she wished she had. At least he'd know.

Nee, she'd been right not to tell him. Knowing she loved him would be one more burden for Levi, and she didn't want that for him. Especially if she died. She didn't want to leave him with that kind of guilt.

The gun dug deeper into her back as she tripped over an uneven patch of concrete.

"Careful," the man growled in her ear.

There was something familiar about the voice, but she couldn't place it. Billy, Tammy and Pete were all in police custody. Who else could it possibly be? Her mind whirled as she tried to place it. She couldn't think of anyone. Maybe it was one of Jacob's clients. That would make sense, that someone he knew in his business would be connected to the evil that he was trying to shut down.

"I didn't expect that your friend would know how to drive," the voice continued. "I planned on shooting the cop, then you'd be easy to grab. Your guy messed up my plans."

Odd. There was almost a grudging respect there, as if Levi's quick thinking and unusual skill with vehicles had earned his admiration.

What a foolish idea.

The man edged her off the main street and down an empty alley.

Her fear ratcheted up a notch. She could smell her own terror. It stung her nostrils.

"Hurry up." The gun twisted. She gasped, her back stinging.

Would she die here, now that they were away from any witnesses?

But her captor didn't stop or shoot her. Instead, he continued to shove her in front of him, marching her on to some place only he knew.

What would Levi think when he came back and found she was missing? Had anyone seen her leave?

Her feet began to ache. She didn't dare complain, though. If she could stay alive, maybe there was hope that Levi could find her. His boss had a phone. Levi could call the police, and they would come. Officer Dawson, she was sure, would immediately realize that she was in trouble. She just had to stay alive.

How long had they been walking? Fifteen minutes? Twenty?

Levi's tours lasted from forty-five minutes to an hour. He wouldn't be back yet. No one knew she was missing. Not yet.

The man suddenly dragged her sideways.

There, parked at the end of the forlorn alley, was an undistinguished four-door sedan. It was gray. She'd seen similar cars on the road frequently. Nothing about this vehicle stood out.

It was deliberate, she knew.

Suddenly, the hope she'd been carrying withered.

Even if they searched, they wouldn't know about this car. Unlike the green Jeep that Officer Dawson knew about, this car would blend in seamlessly.

He stopped at the back of the car. She began to turn toward her captor. The gun was removed from her back and she saw an arm lift.

Raising her arms instinctively to protect herself, she backed away a step.

The gun gleamed as it was brought down and smashed against the side of her head.

She was out before she hit the ground.

SIXTEEN

She couldn't see anything. The small, enclosed space she found herself trapped in was a dark, inky black. A stale, moldy odor wafted past her nostrils. She gagged. Her mouth was covered with some kind of tape, probably duct tape.

Shifting, she attempted to get her hands free. That was when she realized her feet were tied together at the ankles. Her arms had been tethered behind her back. She wiggled, seeing if she could free them. The movement sent pain darting through her head.

She became aware of something sticky on her face. Blood.

The memories flooded back. She had waited for Levi while he had been working. Someone came up behind her and forced her to move at gunpoint. When he stopped at his car and she had started to whirl to face the person, she had been struck on the temple.

The floor beneath her cheek vibrated. Suddenly, she realized that she was stuffed in a car trunk and being taken somewhere. For a moment hope bloomed. Maybe they didn't plan on killing her.

The hope died as she thought about other things that could happen to her.

Levi was her one hope. Would he find her? A sob tore at her throat. How could he possibly find her? She was taken when he was gone, and they hadn't figured out who the sniper was, or who had hired Tammy to set the fires. Unless her abductor had left an obvious clue, she didn't see how Levi or Officer Dawson would be able to find her.

Her only hope was to pray. She was so weary, even praying seemed to take too much energy. She settled her head down on the metallic surface. Tears leaked out of her eyes and slipped to the trunk.

Please, Gott. *Please.*

The vibrations slowly rocked her to sleep.

She lifted her head and blinked blearily against the sunlight as the trunk popped open. A man leaned down and dragged her out of the trunk. She couldn't make out his face yet. Those hours in the trunk and the bright sunlight had her vision confused. All she saw was a dark hulking form. His hands on her arms were hard. He swung her up over his shoulder and carried her into a building.

As her vision became acclimated to the light, she noticed her surroundings. She was in some kind of store. Antiques were all around her. He led her past the merchandise, through a long hallway and then into a back room. It looked like a smaller version of the store. She saw more antiques, although they weren't placed in any order. This must have been where they brought the antiques before displaying them.

Before she could take further stock of this room, he hauled her back over his shoulder and dropped her on the ceramic tile floor like a sack of potatoes. Her wrists protested her rough treatment and she ached where her tailbone connected with the floor.

Glaring, she faced her abductor.

"Owen!" She couldn't believe it. The funny driver Levi had hired was the man who had taken her.

A moan over in the corner drew her attention. Hannah. She was pale and her eyes were rimmed with red. But she was alive. Even as Lilah watched, her sister-in-law's face contorted in pain and she began to pant.

"Hannah!"

"Lilah…" Hannah moaned. "The *boppli* is coming early."

The blood curdled in her veins. The *boppli* couldn't have picked a worse time to make his or her appearance.

"I love family reunions, don't you?"

Lilah shifted her attention back to Owen. He seemed so normal. She would never have guessed him as the leader of the drug ring. Never.

"Why?"

There were so many questions in that one word. Why had he killed Jacob? Kidnapped Hannah? Shot at her and Levi? Destroyed Jacob's office? The list went on. It was too overwhelming to mentally sort through it all.

"Why?" He sneered. "Your brother was going to destroy me. For four years, I supplied him with the drugs he needed to support his addiction. He was in pain—I helped him out. It was a business! Then I get a frantic call from Billy, one of my, ah, shall we say, business associates. Billy saw Jacob in a meeting and recognized the gentleman as the cop who'd arrested him earlier. So, I confronted Jacob. He had gone to the police and was going to hand over evidence he'd gathered against me. He planned to demolish me. I offered him money. All I needed was for him to hand over the evidence he'd collected. But Jacob wouldn't deal. He had a family. He couldn't be a part of my 'evil' business."

Owen made air quotes with his fingers. He speared her with a hard glare. She shuddered. His eyes were full of menace and hate.

"I needed to take care of him, so I hired Tammy to set the fire. Arson is her specialty. She did a good job. It would have all been fine, but then you got nosy. I was at the house the day of the funeral. I heard you when his wife kicked you out. You were going to snoop. I knew you'd be more familiar with where your brother kept things. I had to stop you."

She stared at him, appalled at what he was saying. In one corner of her brain, she knew he planned to kill both she and Hannah. Otherwise, he wouldn't tell them anything.

"And then she started asking questions," he pointed his thumb at Hannah. "When the police said that the fire was arson, she started trying to find out who it was."

A phone rang in the store beyond.

Owen's mouth twisted. "Don't go away."

He stalked out.

"Lilah."

Hannah's voice was soft and pleading. "I was trying to protect you. When I kicked you out, I knew I was going to try and get answers. Jacob had loved you and tried to protect you. I couldn't look until you were out of danger. Jacob would have wanted me to keep you safe."

With those words, Lilah forgave everything. All the pain and all the distress had been unimportant. There were so many things she wanted to say to Hannah.

"Hannah—"

But she couldn't say anything else. Owen stormed back into the room, his face like a thundercloud.

"Where is it?" he shouted at Lilah. "I talked with one of my dealers. The cops have finally left your place. My guys went there and found everything had been dug up. I know they found it! Where is his box? The one your brother was going to turn in to the police. I know you and your boyfriend have it. I want what was inside! Where are the pictures? The receipts?"

He grabbed a large vase from the counter and slammed it to the floor. Shards of glass flew out in every direction. He toppled over a cabinet. It landed on Lilah's ankle. She screamed in agony.

*   *   *

Levi paced the conference room at the police station. Lilah had been gone for three hours. Three hours! Anything could have happened to her in that time. He spun around to escape from the violence of his thoughts.

Why had he left her alone? If he had been with her, he could have stopped this from happening.

Maybe. His chin dropped to his chest. He was Amish now, and no longer carried a gun. Never again would he point a weapon at another person. Nor would he ever want to. So, if Lilah's kidnapper had come at them, he wouldn't have shot him or her.

But he would have stood between her and any enemy who tried to hurt her without caring about the risk. Even if it meant taking a bullet.

But he hadn't been there.

Officer Dawson charged into the room, holding a paper high in the air.

"We've got 'em!" She slapped the paper on the table. "Owen Brown."

Levi staggered. "Owen? He drives Amish people around."

"He does. Billy Whitman rolled on him. Once we had a name, we were able to dig up lots of other interesting information on him.

Like the fact that he also deals in illegal narcotic sales, including to students at the local high school. Several of his dealers are kids he blackmailed into working for him. His latest venture has been into the world of human trafficking. Six months ago, several women in Ohio and Pennsylvania were reported missing, and authorities had reason to believe they'd been taken by force. Just last night, one of them managed to escape and returned to Pennsylvania. She came forward and identified Owen as one of her captors. She had heard them talking about selling the women. As we speak, a drawing is being distributed to other precincts in the area. There's a BOLO out for him."

For the first time in the past three hours, a kernel of hope nestled in his heart. He held tight to that hope for the next ninety minutes.

Another officer entered the room and reported that Owen Brown had been spotted entering an antique shop owned by his aunt.

Five minutes later, Levi was in the car with Officer Dawson, heading east to save Lilah. Two other cruisers had been dispatched to the same location. They were going in without lights or sirens. No sense in warning Owen that they were coming.

"He must have been the sniper," Levi guessed. "Did he have any training?"

"Yes." She cast a glance in the rearview mirror. "He had gone into the service but had been dishonorably discharged when he swung at his commanding officer. He didn't serve any jail time."

Levi processed this new information. "He had to have seen me at Lilah's *haus* that first day when we went to search through what had been her brother's office. When I called him to drive us to Hannah's *haus*, I think he was trying to figure out how much we knew."

She agreed. He sat tensely beside her, every moment dragging. Finally, they pulled into the alley behind the antique shop. When she left the car, Levi sat for a moment, then he followed. He needed to be there when Lilah was found.

He entered the shop. No one was there. Near the back of the store, he saw a hallway. Moving on silent feet, he turned into the hallway and saw Officer Dawson. She frowned when she saw him, her gaze grew steely. He'd have some explaining to do, but he didn't care.

A sharp cry came from behind the door. A woman was behind the door and she was in agony.

Lilah was going to die if he didn't get in there.

Levi kicked in the door and rushed into the room, ignoring Officer Dawson's shout. The door banged against the wall and bounced back, knocking him in the side of the head. He barely even noticed. All his attention was focused on the terrified blonde sitting on the floor against the opposite wall. Vaulting over the countertop, he rushed Owen.

Owen raised the gun to fire, but he was too late. Levi hit him with enough force to send the gun flying.

Officer Dawson entered the room behind him, her weapon drawn and held high, centered on Owen's chest. Levi knew she'd probably yell at him later, but he didn't care. Lilah was alive. Obviously injured, but she would be well. Nothing mattered to him except that.

"Down on the ground!" Officer Dawson shouted.

Instead of complying, Owen backed up and turned to run, his feet skidding on the slippery tiles. He was running toward the back door. Levi knew if he made it out that door, he'd be going straight into the parking lot. What chance did he have of making it to his vehicle to get away?

The police officers who had piled into the room behind Officer Dawson surrounded him.

Levi ran to Lilah and dropped to his knees beside her, barely aware of the jolt as he hit the hard ceramic tiles.

"Are you hurt anywhere?" He visually scanned her from head to toe, trying to find any serious injuries. She was bruised and scratched, and she would probably have a black eye within a couple of hours. But to his relief, he couldn't see any other injuries.

"My ankle. The cabinet fell on it, but I don't think it's serious."

He nodded. "We should let someone look at it. Just to be sure it's okay."

"I'm fine," she gasped. "Hannah. Hannah is not well. I think she's going into labor."

He had been so focused on Lilah that he hadn't paid much attention to Hannah, where she was huddled against the wall in the corner. He looked at her now. She was pale, shivering, and she was definitely in pain. Even while he watched, her face twisted in agony. She was having trouble catching a full breath.

What really worried him though was the water pooled around her.

There was no doubt about it. Hannah was definitely in labor. And if her water had broken as he suspected, there was no stopping it. That *boppli* was coming, whether they were ready or not.

"Lilah, I need to go check her out. I'll be right back."

"I understand. Do what you can for her."

Despite her brave words, he saw the terror in her eyes. When he hesitated, however, she shoved him away. "Go! She needs you."

That was the moment Levi finally stopped fighting against his heart. He loved this sweet, brave woman who put those she cared about above herself. Always. He didn't know if he could ever be worthy of her, but he was so sick of trying to fight against it. If she would have him, he intended to make her his wife.

Quickly, he ducked and kissed her forehead before running across the room and checking on Hannah. He squatted down beside her. He didn't like the red spot across her shoulder. He was no doctor, but he was pretty certain she was going to need medical care, possibly even surgery. He hoped an ambulance was already on the way.

"Hannah, can you hear me?"

"Hurts," she panted. "Hurts. *Boppli* is too soon."

Grimly, he reached his hand out and felt the

pulse of her wrist. It was strong. Rapid, but that wasn't surprising, considering what she was going through.

A sudden bellow rent the room. Levi spun on his heels. Owen was grappling with an officer. A chill went through Levi when Owen's hand touched the service weapon at the officer's waist. Hatred shone from his narrowed glance as it lasered in on Lilah.

"Your fault!" he shouted, spittle bubbling in the corners of his mouth. "This is all your fault."

Levi knew what was going to happen. He shouted and barged across the room.

Too late. Owen wrenched the gun out of the weapon belt and took a wild shot at Lilah.

She cried out. For a single moment, Levi imagined that her cry was one of fear, that Owen had missed her. Then Lilah grabbed her thigh with both hands. The spreading stain beneath them made Levi sick to his stomach. He fought against the nightmare that threatened to hurl him back in time and render him useless to Lilah.

It only took a second or two for him to reach her side, but she was already pale, and her teeth were chattering.

"Stay with me, Lilah. Stay with me." His

words tumbled out of his mouth, shaking and shivering as if he'd been sitting in a freezer.

He shut the rest of the room out. He heard Owen crying and wailing as he was put on the ground, handcuffed and had his rights read to him. He knew another officer was tending to Hannah.

It didn't matter.

He took the end of Lilah's skirt where it had torn, probably caught on something, and tore a strip off.

Officer Dawson dropped down beside him.

"Two ambulances are on the way," she rasped, her breathing harsh.

"I need to stop the bleeding. Do you have anything I can use, other than my hands I mean," he snapped. "She's losing too much blood."

She nodded. "You keep pressure on the wound. I have a first aid kit in the cruiser."

She ran out before he could respond. He kept pressure on Lilah's leg. Even though his right arm wasn't as strong or flexible as his left, he was still more than capable of using it effectively enough to do first aid on the woman he loved more than anything.

He didn't know what he'd do if she died.

"*Gott.* Help me. Help her. Please, *Gott.* Give me the wisdom to do what I need to do."

Officer Dawson sprinted through the door and swung a first aid bag down. She opened it and efficiently pulled out the supplies they needed. Working as a team, they used the clean pads and applied pressure to stem the bleeding. Sweat broke out on Levi's head as the second pad soaked through. Officer Dawson handed him another one. He placed it on top of the other two, pressing down on the wound, wincing when Lilah whimpered and tossed her head.

"I know it hurts, Lilah. We have to stop the bleeding." He remained focused on his task. "I won't let you die."

Silent tears were running down her cheeks. At some point, her lids had fallen closed. "Lilah, wake up. You need to stay awake."

She moved slightly, her lids fluttering.

"So hard. Want to sleep…" She slurred her words. His heartbeat went into overdrive. He couldn't lose her now.

"*Nee!* Lilah Schwartz, don't you give up. Stay with me, do you hear me? I'm not going to lose you."

"Levi—"

"*Jah,* I'm here! I'm always going to be here."

Her lids fluttered a few more times before she dragged them open. It was obviously an effort for her. Her eyes were hazy.

"Levi, you're blurry."

He swiped his arm across his face to clear away the tears blocking his own vision. "*Jah*, I know. Hold on."

Sirens were coming closer. "Lilah, I hear the ambulances. You're going to be okay. Just hold on a little longer."

He couldn't keep the ragged sob constricting his throat at bay. She lifted a hand and traced it down his cheek. "Don't cry. Doesn't hurt anymore."

That was not a good sign.

The paramedics entered and took over. He was edged out of the way. Officer Dawson stood with him while Lilah and Hannah were strapped to stretchers and carried out to the ambulances.

Owen was gone, too, on his way to the hospital.

Levi swallowed the rage inside him. It had all been about greed. Jacob had died, and Hannah and Lilah were seriously injured, because of greed.

"Levi." Officer Dawson placed a hand on

his elbow. "Come on. You can ride with me to the hospital."

He followed her out to her cruiser. He didn't speak during the drive, too overcome with his emotions to hold on to the threads of a conversation. She seemed to understand.

"Hold on, Levi. I'll get us there as fast as I can."

He couldn't respond, his throat was tight, and he felt as though he'd been hollowed out. If anything happened to Lilah—

He wouldn't go there. Squeezing his eyes shut, Levi dug deep and prayed for all he was worth. He prayed for Hannah. He prayed for the *boppli*. But most of all, he prayed for Lilah. He prayed for that beautiful girl with the blond hair and deep blue eyes, who had managed to pull him out of his self-imposed isolation from his emotions.

Officer Dawson flipped on the siren and the lights. Levi appreciated it. Anything that would get him to the hospital sooner.

The cars in front of them sheared off to the side of the road, letting them pass.

"We'll be there in five minutes. Six, tops," Officer Dawson told him, her knuckles white on the steering wheel.

It was going to be a very long five minutes.

SEVENTEEN

Levi followed the stretcher carrying Lilah into the hospital. He stuck close until the hospital staff stopped him. Helpless, his eyes tracked her as she was borne through double doors that swung shut behind her. Lost, he wandered around the waiting room.

A nurse came out from behind the registration counter, a tablet and stylus pen in hand. He responded to her questions, impatience making his skin itch. He wanted to bust through the doors to see where she was.

What if she died? There had been so much blood. Leg wounds were tricky. He had no idea if the bullet had nicked the artery or not. He had stemmed the bleeding as much as he could, but she'd lost so much before the ambulance and paramedics had arrived to take over. He didn't think he'd ever erase the memory of her lying so still and pale from his mind.

Had he done enough, fast enough?

His mind swam with one horrid outcome after another. He shook his head, trying to literally shake the thoughts from his mind. It was pointless to stand here considering the worst-case scenario. And almost as pointless, to his way of thinking, was answering these questions when Lilah was fighting for her life.

"Sir, who is her next of kin?"

"What?" he frowned at the nurse. "Next of kin? Not sure. She had lived with her brother, but he was recently killed in a fire. Her sister-in-law was brought in about the same time as Lilah. She was in premature labor."

Her entire family was either dead or in the hospital with her. Lilah had no one.

Nee. That wasn't completely true.

Lilah had him. Levi needed to stay strong and steady. At least until she was on the mend. His stomach dropped at the idea of his world without her.

Breathing deep, he fought down the despair. Lilah would make it. She was young and strong. The doctors would know what to do for her. She would recover.

Then what? He couldn't think of leaving her. He couldn't do it. But would it be selfish to stay? He loved her, but would it be enough?

He still had issues he was working through. Nightmares and flashbacks.

He finished answering the nurse's questions. When she left him alone, he prowled along the edges of the room, his mind churning and boiling with doubts and fears.

What would Lilah do if she had been in his place? He knew the answer before he'd finished asking the question. She would pray.

In the empty waiting room, Levi bowed his head and prayed. He prayed for the sweet woman in surgery. He prayed for Hannah and her *boppli*. And he prayed for himself, that *Gott* would reveal His wisdom.

Levi had no idea how long he stood in that room, pouring out his heart to *Gott*, begging for His healing touch on the woman who held his heart in her slender hands. By the time he finished, more people had filtered in.

He glanced at the clock on the wall. It was nearly eleven thirty. He had been in the waiting room for nearly two hours. And still no word.

A hand landed on his shoulder. Startled, Levi turned his head.

"Aiden! What are you doing here?"

He wiped his hand across his eyes.

"Your brother Abram called me. Told me what was going on. I left the minute I heard."

Aiden lived several hours away. Levi had no problem believing the man he'd gone to war with would drop everything to come to his aid. That was the kind of man he was. Levi would do the same for him. "Aw, man. You didn't have to do that. But I'm glad to see you."

Aiden flashed him a tight grin. "No sweat. I remember many times when you dropped what you were doing to help me. Have you heard anything?"

"Not yet." A doctor entered the room, her surgical mask pulled down under her chin. Her eyes scanned the room and rested on him. "I think we're about to," Levi murmured.

He swiveled on his heels until he was standing next to his friend, hands clasped behind his back, legs spread slightly, falling back on his military training for support.

"Mr. Burkholder?"

He nodded. He couldn't have spoken if he'd tried. His mouth was as dry as the Sahara. His throat felt like he'd swallowed a large cotton ball.

"Your friend, Lilah Schwartz, is out of surgery and resting. You should be able to see her in about an hour."

He swallowed. "Will she be fine?"

The surgeon smiled. "She will. We stopped

the bleeding. We needed to do a graft to repair the artery, but it was barely scratched. Her ankle needed a couple of pins. She'll be unable to walk for a few weeks, but she will heal. I don't want her to be alone."

"She can stay with my family until she heals."

The doctor smiled.

"What about her sister-in-law? Hannah Schwartz?"

"The baby is fine. So is Hannah. She had a little girl. We'll keep the baby here for a week or so, but she's breathing on her own."

When the doctor left, Levi wilted into a chair. He held the bridge of his nose and focused on breathing, striving to keep the tears filling his eyes at bay.

She was fine. They would all live.

"Hey, buddy. You okay?" Aiden settled into the chair beside Levi. It creaked when he shifted his weight.

"I honestly don't know." Levi leaned forward. "I could use some guidance here."

Aiden smiled. "Let me guess. You're in love and about to do something really stupid."

Levi scowled at his best friend. "I didn't ask to be insulted." He leaned back in his chair. "Define *stupid*."

Aiden grinned. "*Stupid* is thinking that the

girl who means the world to you would be better off without you. Seriously. Dude. How many women did God make that would be perfect for you, even with all your flaws?"

One. He made one.

Levi nodded. "*Jah*, I get what you're saying. How did you know what I was considering?"

Aiden gave a one-shouldered shrug, grimacing. "How do you think? I made the same idiotic decision when I realized I was falling for Sophie."

"What?"

Several people shushed him. He hadn't meant to shout.

"What?" he repeated with less volume.

"You heard me." Aiden tilted his head. "You remember when I brought her to you. She and Celine. Man, she was messing with my head, even after only a day. It wasn't long before I knew she was the one for me. But I was stubborn. I refused to commit. I had too much baggage. Too many issues. All sorts of lies."

"Are they lies?" Levi broke in.

Aiden stared him straight in the eye. "Every single excuse I told myself was just that. An excuse. Yes, I had baggage. But so did she. I had issues from my childhood. She was dealing with her family's death and her uncle's ultimate betrayal. That's life. You still go on, learn to cope."

Levi mulled his friend's words in his mind. Could he be right?

"I want to believe you."

"Listen, Levi, I know it's hard. Tell me this. Do you believe God can do anything? Really believe?"

"*Jah*, I do."

"Then why are you doubting that He could make a woman who will accept all your human flaws?"

Why indeed?

"So, my next question is, can I come to your wedding? You know Sophie will want to meet your Lilah."

Levi laughed, the burden of his own inadequacies lifted from his soul. *Gott* was enough. He would make up for what Levi lacked.

"I haven't even asked her yet. Ask me if she says yes. I haven't told her I love her yet."

"You will."

"I will."

Aiden bumped his shoulder with his fist. "I'm thinking positive. When she says yes, I plan to be there to see you hitched. Might even wear a suit and tie."

Levi chuckled, shaking his head. "If she

agrees to be my wife, then *jah*, of course you will be invited. I'd ask you to be my best man, but that's the *Englisch* way. You won't be able to sit with the community, but I would be disappointed if you weren't there."

"Mr. Burkholder?"

Levi's head snapped up. He and Aiden had been so busy talking, the nurse had sneaked up on them. *"Jah?"*

He held his breath.

"The doctor said that you can go in and see Miss Schwartz for a few minutes. She needs her rest, and she might be a little sleepy from the anesthesia and pain medication, but you can see her if you'll follow me."

He was out of his seat before she completed speaking. Blood pounded in his ears. He knew what he wanted. What he didn't know was whether she shared the same dream.

"Lilah? Can you hear me?"

Levi's voice came to her through the fog clouding her mind. Her eyes were glued shut. She couldn't open them. She had to. What if he went away?

Struggling, she fought her way to the surface, peeling her lids open. Everything was blurry. She blinked several times, clearing her vision. The room came into view slowly. She was in a hospital room. Her breathing sped up as she recalled being shot.

"Lilah."

Turning her head on the pillow, her gaze met Levi's. Deep furrows creased his forehead. They cleared as he stared at her.

"I was starting to get worried." He reached out his left hand and stroked a finger down her cheek. "You wouldn't wake up."

She was distracted by his gentle touch. "Hannah?"

Her voice rose when she thought about her sister-in-law. Hannah had been injured.

"Shh." He tried to calm her. "Hannah is well. And so is her daughter."

She'd had her baby. She fluttered her lashes to clear the tears forming. "Jacob has a daughter."

A sweet little girl he'd never get a chance to meet. But his daughter was alive, and his wife was well. That would be all that mattered to Jacob.

She sighed. How was it possible to be so happy and yet so sad at the same time? Happy because her family had survived the horror of the past few days. She would praise *Gott* forever for that blessing. There had been several times that she hadn't believed that they would all make it out alive. But He had proven once again that He was in charge.

At the same time, however, there was a deep sorrow spiraling down in her soul. Lilah had been aware that Levi was pulling back. From the moment he kissed her, his withdrawal had been evident. She knew he had feelings for her. Just as she had feelings for him. She didn't think it would be enough. Something inside him was broken. More than just a physical injury.

"I only have a few minutes, Lilah. I won't be able to tell you everything now."

Here it comes. Levi was going to tell her that they would never work out. He was walking out of her life. Lilah braced herself. She'd tried to pretend that she would be fine without him, but it wasn't true. Her heart would always bear a Levi-shaped hole if he left her.

"Say what you must. I'm tired."

He hesitated. The light was funny in the room. His face seemed pale.

He sucked in a deep breath. "I love you."

She blinked. "What?"

"I knew I wouldn't get this right," he growled.

"Wait!" She struggled to sit up. Pain shot through her leg. Falling back, she groaned. Levi leaned over her. Tears blurred his face.

He grabbed her hand. "It's *gut*. I'm not leaving. Not until the nurse comes back and kicks me out."

"Say it again. I must have heard you wrong."

He stepped closer to the bed and squeezed her hand. "You didn't hear me wrong. I love you."

She sighed. "I was sure you were going to tell me you didn't want to see me anymore."

"I almost did," he admitted, his voice a low rumble.

She knew he'd changed his mind. Otherwise he wouldn't be here now telling her he loved her. Levi was not a man who would play with a woman's affections that way. Still, the knowledge that he had considered walking away from her hurt. She rubbed at her chest, trying to ease the pain.

"I'm sorry," he whispered. "I forgot to trust *Gott*. I had convinced myself that my flaws made me unlovable."

"You are lovable," she exclaimed. "You're honest, hardworking and kind of quirky! You are also so strong."

One eyebrow lifted in response to her last claim.

"I don't know how true that is, but *danke*."

She scowled at him. "*Jah*, you are strong. You have been through war, lost an arm, and in the last few days, you have kept me, and then Hannah and her *boppli*, safe from a killer."

His eyes brightened. He dropped his gaze. She watched a slow tide of red swarm up his neck and face.

"Levi."

She waited until he raised his head and looked at her again. "I know you still have nightmares. I know you sometimes struggle with the things you had to do while you were *Englisch*. I ache for what you suffered, but I don't think poorly of you because of it." She could do this. "I love you, too."

He stepped closer to the bed, his eyes devouring her face. "*Jah?* You're sure?"

"*Jah*. More than ever."

"Would you consider walking out with me?" he asked.

She smiled. He wanted to court her. She wanted more than that, but they had time. Now that a killer no longer hunted her.

"*Jah*. I will walk out with you. Gladly."

His left hand moved up to cup her cheek. "*Gut*. Then after a few weeks, I'll probably ask for your hand in marriage."

She laughed, a soft breathy sound.

"Why don't you ask me now, since you have already decided you will?"

He shook his head. "*Nee.* I will do this the right way."

"*Jah?* So, if you ask me to marry you this fall, will we get married before Christmas?" She hoped so.

"Of course. In late October or early November. Unless you want to wait?"

"*Nee!*" She narrowed her eyes. "I have waited long enough for you, Levi Burkholder. I want to be your *frau* as soon as possible."

"I promised Aiden he could come to our wedding," he murmured, his hand clasping hers. "He told me I'd be a fool to let you go. I agree. I don't know what I was thinking."

"I look forward to meeting your friend."

Gently, slowly, he leaned down and pressed his lips to hers. Her heart pounded in her veins. Her lips tingled after he moved back. "I will do my best to be a *gut ehemann.*"

"You will be," she assured him. "*Gott* has brought us together for a reason. Hopefully, someday soon, He'll bless us with *kinder* to raise.*"

He bent to kiss her again. Before their lips touched, the door swung open. Levi straightened. Lilah tried to appear calm, despite the heat pooling in her cheeks. She didn't need a mirror to know they were as red as the lipstick on the nurse who entered. The amused look she swung between them confirmed Lilah's suspicion.

"Time's up!" she sang. "Visiting hours will start again tomorrow morning at nine. You can come back and see your friend then."

Levi nodded. "*Jah*. I will be back."

Lilah touched his hand. She needed to make sure they were in agreement before he left. Otherwise she'd worry about it all night until he arrived in the morning. "He's not my friend. This is my fiancé."

Levi met her eyes and grinned. She grinned back when he didn't argue. She was engaged. Bubbles of happiness buzzed around inside her. She was floating, she was so happy.

"Well congratulations, kids!" The nurse smiled. "I'm happy for you both. Now go, Mr. Fiancé. Your sweetheart needs her rest if she's going to get well enough to meet you at church for your wedding."

Levi swooped down and kissed her cheek before tossing a jaunty wave at the nurse and leaving. Lilah sank back against her pillow. The nurse bustled around the room, but Lilah barely noticed. Her mind was occupied with thoughts of Levi and what kind of life they would have together.

She could hardly wait for it to begin.

EPILOGUE

Three years later

Lilah gave the soup simmering on the stove a final stir. Tapping the wooden spoon against the edge of the large pot to remove the excess liquid, she put the utensil back on the ceramic spoon rest. The house already smelled like apples and cinnamon from the pies she and Hannah had baked that afternoon. They had spent a lovely two hours picking apples yesterday. It had been quite an undertaking with the children, but Lilah had enjoyed every chaotic moment. Tomorrow, she'd can the rest to make applesauce and spiced apples to eat through the rest of the year.

She cast a glance at the clock on the wall. Levi would be home soon. Her pulse sped up as it usually did when she thought of her handsome husband. They'd been married almost two and a half years, and she thanked *Gott* every day for blessing her with so much.

Grabbing the broom, she hummed as she swept the floor. It gave her so much pleasure making the *haus* spotless for Levi. Setting the broom aside, she cast her glance around, making sure everything was perfect. The kitchen floor was clean enough to eat off, the countertops gleamed. The kitchen opened into the living room. From where she stood, she had a clear view of the next room. Sighing, she hugged herself. She could hardly believe this was her *haus*.

Normally, they would have moved into Levi's parents' *haus* since he was the eldest son, and his parents would have moved to the *dawdi haus*, a small *haus* next to the main one. However, Levi and his *daed* had decided it would make more sense for one of Levi's brothers to take that *haus* and take over David's business when it was time. Both of his brothers had joined the family painting business. Although Levi helped them from time to time, he had no interest in painting full-time.

Lilah didn't mind. Levi had given up his job driving buggies and was now dividing his time between working as a carpenter and earning a few extra dollars as a mechanic. When he'd announced they wouldn't be moving in with his family, she'd wondered where they would live.

He'd surprised her with plans for their own *haus*. He'd sold the *haus* that he and Aiden had built years before, along with the ten acres of land. The money the sale had brought in, combined with the money he'd saved up, had been enough for him to buy land locally. He had called in his brothers, his *daed* and his buddy Aiden to build the two-story structure.

Lilah had enjoyed spending time with Aiden's pretty wife, Sophie, and her sister, Celine, even though it had been difficult to keep from peeking to check on the progress the men were making. One thing that had helped keep her occupied was watching Sophie's daughter, Rose, and her baby, Brian.

Hannah had come out with her sister to join them twice that week. Tears stung her eyes. Jacob would have loved seeing his wife and sister becoming true friends at last. He would have been a wonderful father to his daughter. Adele was a precocious three-year-old now. Hannah still lived with her parents, but probably would be moving out soon. She had admitted to Lilah that she was being courted by a young man in her district. Lilah had caught her breath, but she'd been happy for her friend.

Hannah was lovely and had much to offer, both as a wife and as a mother. It would be good for Adele to have siblings.

Hannah had sold the property where she had lived with Jacob and Lilah. She had told Lilah she'd never be able to live in a *haus* built on that land again.

A buggy pulled onto the driveway. Brushing her fingertips under her eyes, she smeared away the dampness collected on her lashes. She darted through the large opening into the living room and went to the blanket spread out on the floor.

"Harrison, your *daed* is home!"

The thirteen-month-old chucked his blocks away and stood on his chubby little legs. He toddled over to Lilah. "*Daed* home. *Daed* home."

Swooping down, she gathered him in her arms and pressed a kiss on his cheek. "Let's go meet him on the porch, *jah*?"

Harrison wasn't a typical Amish name. But when Levi had asked if they could name their *boppli* for his friend who had once saved his life in Afghanistan and had never made it home, she had agreed that it was a fine name. Her little man looked exactly like she imagined Levi would have looked as a *boppli*. Stepping onto the porch, she lifted her head and smiled as a cool breeze brushed her cheeks. The air was thick with the scent of wood smoke and changing leaves.

She loved this time of year.

Opening her eyes, Lilah watched as Levi left the barn where he'd put the mare. He saw them on the porch. His face lit up, sparking a flutter in her heart. The air of loneliness that had surrounded him when they'd met was long gone. He still suffered from occasional nightmares, but had not a flashback since they'd wed. Another blessing.

"How's my best girl?" Levi jogged up the steps to join them on the porch. He enfolded them into his embrace. "Hi, buddy. How's my guy?" He plopped a kiss on Harrison's curly blond hair. The kiss he gave his wife was much longer. Harrison started to squirm in Lilah's arms. Laughing, Levi stepped back and took his son into the crook of his left arm. Together, they returned to the *haus*. The moment they entered, Levi closed his eyes and inhaled deeply.

"Mmm. Something smells *gut*, Lilah." He sniffed again. "Apple pie?"

She grinned. He was like a *kinder*. "*Jah*. We

have ice cream, too. And ham and bean soup with corn bread for dinner."

He leaned down and kissed her again. "You take *wunderbar* care of us, Lilah Burkholder."

She could say the same of him. Not only had he provided her with a roof over her head in a spectacular way, his love and faith in her had helped her to overcome her insecurities. No longer did she blame herself for Jacob's death or the choices he had made. He had been a victim, but he had made those choices without consulting her.

After dinner, Levi helped her put Harrison to bed. They walked hand in hand back to the living room and looked out the large picture window together.

"I have something to tell you. I hope you won't mind." He kissed the top of her head.

She twisted her neck slightly to peer up at him. "What would I mind?"

She wasn't worried. Not really. Levi had never let her down. She trusted his judgment.

"I was approached today by one of the Weaver brothers. He asked me if I'd be interested in being nominated for the vacant minister position."

She sucked in a breath, shocked. It was indeed an honor to be nominated for such a position, but the role took an immense amount of time and energy, without any compensation. She pushed the worry away. If it was *Gott*'s will, that was all there was to it.

"What did you tell him?"

He shrugged, a smile playing around his lips. "I told him, *danke*, I appreciate the honor. And if he really feels strongly about it, I wouldn't say no."

"But?" she prompted.

He nodded. "But, if he wasn't set on it, I would just as well forgo the honor. After all, I have a young family to care for."

He put his left arm around her and drew her close, kissing her softly in the waning light. She placed a hand on his chest and looked up at him.

"*Jah*, you have a young family. And a rapidly growing one."

He started to nod, then stopped, his dark eyes flaring wide-open. "Lilah?"

She placed a hand on her belly. "Harrison will have a brother or sister in about seven months."

He pulled his arm from around her shoulder and placed his hand over hers. "A *boppli*."

The wonder in his voice made her weepy. Knowing Levi, she had no doubt he'd react strongly with each new *boppli*. She hoped there would be many. She and Levi had talked about a big family. But she would be grateful for the children *Gott* provided, whether there were two or ten.

"Levi Burkholder, I love you so much," she murmured, burrowing into his chest.

He hugged her tightly to him. "I love you, Lilah. You've taken a broken man and made him whole."

She smiled. "We've both been changed, my love. *Gott* knew what He was doing when He had me hide in your barn that day."

He laughed. "*Jah*. He knew I needed you in my life."

He leaned down and kissed her again. Lilah wrapped her arms around her *ehemann* and held on tight to the man who had turned the sorrow in her heart into joy that knew no bounds.

Another *boppli*. Levi could barely wrap his head around the idea. He'd been overjoyed when Lilah had announced she was carrying their first child. It had been more than he'd dared to hope for. He'd not even been sure he could pray for *kinder*, not with his PTSD still affecting his life.

Gott had other plans. And *Gott*'s plans were always the right ones. When he'd held Harrison in his arms, all his fears had melted as love for the squalling bundle filled him. When Harrison had stopped fussing and had snuggled close, Levi had to breathe in deep through his nose to hold in the tears.

His heart swelled in his chest. They were going to be blessed again.

Lilah was staring up at him, her blue eyes loving as they traced his face.

His whole world was right here. He wasn't worried about the nomination. If *Gott* wanted it for him, it would work out.

He was finally content to let go and give it all to *Gott*. Let Him run the show.

Levi tugged Lilah close and held her tight, content. He was right where he needed to be. *Gott*'s plan had been best, after all.

* * * * *

*If you enjoyed this book, don't miss the other
heart-stopping Amish adventures from
Dana R. Lynn's
Amish Country Justice series:*

Plain Target
Plain Retribution
Amish Christmas Abduction
Amish Country Ambush
Amish Christmas Emergency
Guarding the Amish Midwife
Hidden in Amish Country
Plain Refuge
Deadly Amish Reunion

*Available now from Love Inspired Suspense!
Find more great reads at
www.LoveInspired.com.*

Dear Reader,

I hope you enjoyed Levi's and Lilah's journey to their happy-ever-after. It was a pleasure to get to know them as I wrote their story.

Levi was first introduced in *Plain Refuge*. He was a fun secondary character, but I knew he had to have his own story. His strength and his courage masked his brokenness. Lilah had her own share of troubles, but she had no problem seeing the hero in Levi.

I love writing about God's healing grace. This story touched my heart as I wrote it, and I hope it brought you joy.

I love hearing from readers. I can be contacted on my website at www.danarlynn.com, on Facebook at www.facebook.com/WriterDanaLynn or on Instagram at www.instagram.com/DanaRLynn.

Blessings and peace!
Dana R. Lynn

Get 4 FREE REWARDS!

We'll send you 2 FREE Books plus 2 FREE Mystery Gifts.

Love Inspired books feature uplifting stories where faith helps guide you through life's challenges and discover the promise of a new beginning.

FREE
Value Over
$20

YES! Please send me 2 FREE Love Inspired Romance novels and my 2 FREE mystery gifts (gifts are worth about $10 retail). After receiving them, if I don't wish to receive any more books, I can return the shipping statement marked "cancel." If I don't cancel, I will receive 6 brand-new novels every month and be billed just $5.24 each for the regular-print edition or $5.99 each for the larger-print edition in the U.S., or $5.74 each for the regular-print edition or $6.24 each for the larger-print edition in Canada. That's a savings of at least 13% off the cover price. It's quite a bargain! Shipping and handling is just 50¢ per book in the U.S. and $1.25 per book in Canada.* I understand that accepting the 2 free books and gifts places me under no obligation to buy anything. I can always return a shipment and cancel at any time. The free books and gifts are mine to keep no matter what I decide.

Choose one: ☐ **Love Inspired Romance Regular-Print** (105/305 IDN GNWC)   ☐ **Love Inspired Romance Larger-Print** (122/322 IDN GNWC)

Name (please print)

Address   Apt. #

City   State/Province   Zip/Postal Code

Email: Please check this box ☐ if you would like to receive newsletters and promotional emails from Harlequin Enterprises ULC and its affiliates. You can unsubscribe anytime.

Mail to the **Harlequin Reader Service:**
IN U.S.A.: P.O. Box 1341, Buffalo, NY 14240-8531
IN CANADA: P.O. Box 603, Fort Erie, Ontario L2A 5X3

Want to try 2 free books from another series? Call 1-800-873-8635 or visit www.ReaderService.com.

Get 4 FREE REWARDS!

We'll send you 2 FREE Books plus 2 FREE Mystery Gifts.

Harlequin Heartwarming Larger-Print books will connect you to uplifting stories where the bonds of friendship, family and community unite.

FREE Value Over $20

HARLEQUIN SELECTS COLLECTION

19 FREE BOOKS IN ALL!

From Robyn Carr to RaeAnne Thayne to Linda Lael Miller and Sherryl Woods we promise (actually, GUARANTEE!) each author in the Harlequin Selects collection has seen their name on the *New York Times* or *USA TODAY* bestseller lists!

YES! Please send me the **Harlequin Selects Collection**. This collection begins with 3 FREE books and 2 FREE gifts in the first shipment. Along with my 3 free books, I'll also get 4 more books from the Harlequin Selects Collection, which I may either return and owe nothing or keep for the low price of $24.14 U.S./$28.82 CAN. each plus $2.99 U.S./$7.49 CAN. for shipping and handling per shipment*.If I decide to continue, I will get 6 or 7 more books (about once a month for 7 months) but will only need to pay for 4. That means 2 or 3 books in every shipment will be FREE! If I decide to keep the entire collection, I'll have paid for only 32 books because 19 were FREE! I understand that accepting the 3 free books and gifts places me under no obligation to buy anything. I can always return a shipment and cancel at any time. My free books and gifts are mine to keep no matter what I decide.

☐ 262 HCN 5576   ☐ 462 HCN 5576

Name (please print)

Address _____ Apt. #

City _____ State/Province _____ Zip/Postal Code

Mail to the Harlequin Reader Service:
IN U.S.A.: P.O. Box 1341, Buffalo, NY 14240-8531
IN CANADA: P.O. Box 603, Fort Erie, Ontario L2A 5X3

Dana R. Lynn grew up in Illinois. She met her husband at a wedding and told her parents she'd met the man she was going to marry. Nineteen months later, they were married. Today, they live in rural Pennsylvania with their three children and a variety of animals. In addition to writing, she works as a teacher for the deaf and hard of hearing and is active in her church.

Books by Dana R. Lynn

Love Inspired Suspense

Amish Country Justice

Plain Target
Plain Retribution
Amish Christmas Abduction
Amish Country Ambush
Amish Christmas Emergency
Guarding the Amish Midwife
Hidden in Amish Country
Plain Refuge
Deadly Amish Reunion
Amish Country Threats

Visit the Author Profile page at Harlequin.com.

She was standing much too close.

Where was his self-discipline? Distance. He needed distance between him and Lilah.

She was also a woman in danger.

"Here, help me lift that big board on the other side of the tree."

Lilah strode to the other end of the rough wooden plank. Some of the tension bled from his shoulders as the space between them grew wider, allowing him to breathe freely. Together, they heaved the large slab of wood and carried it sideways to a clear spot on the grass.

"*Danke.* Just a few more and we should be all set to go. Easy peasy."

He smiled as a discreet snicker met his ear. *Easy peasy* was a favorite phrase of one of his clients. He'd latched on to several phrases during his time as an *Englischer*.

Lilah straightened, half turned, ready to go back for another board. The grass in front of her feet exploded. A familiar acrid odor rose in the air.

Gunpowder.

Someone was shooting at them.

"Get down!"